A Dress to Die For

Steve Higgs

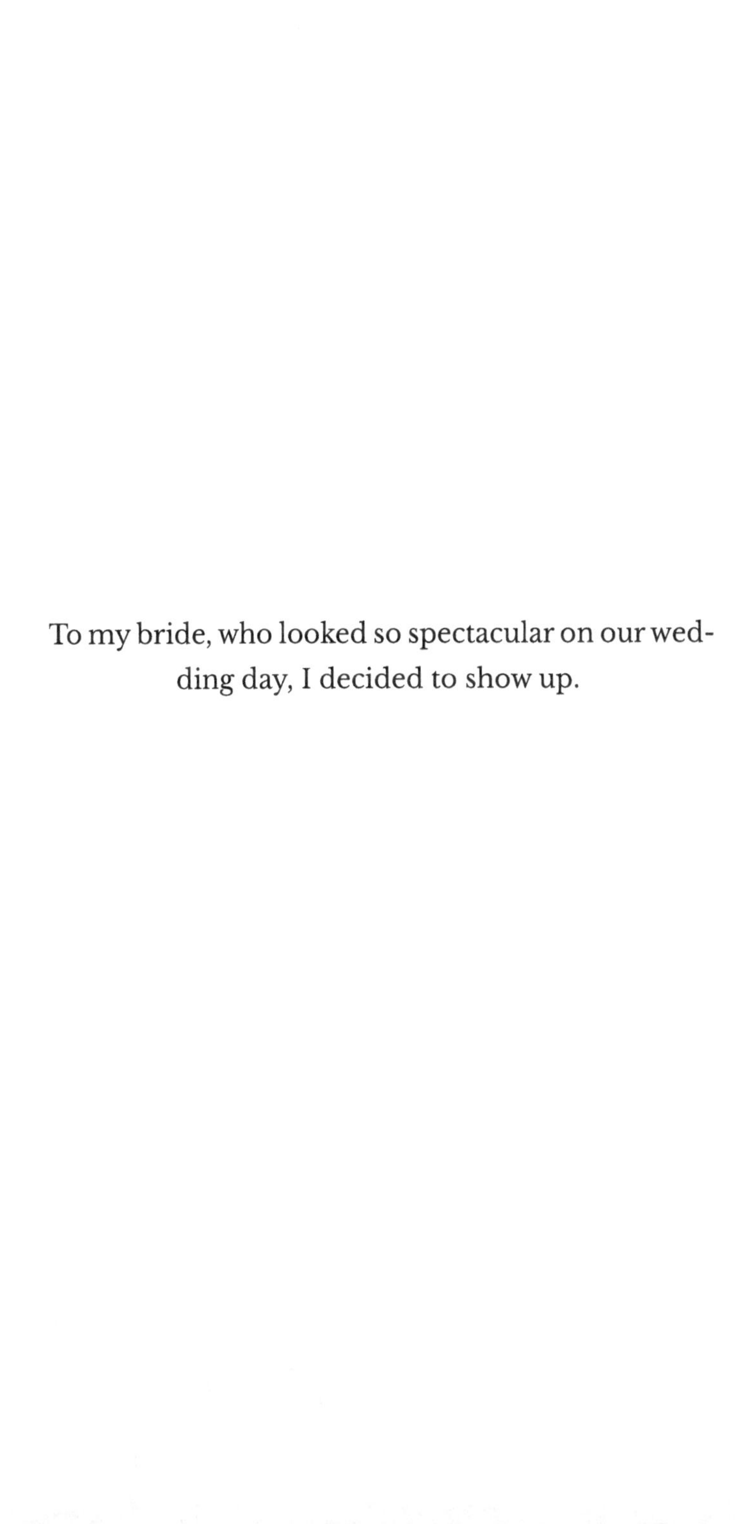

To my bride, who looked so spectacular on our wedding day, I decided to show up.

Contents

NOT THE KIPLING!

The scream shocked me right down to my toes. Not least because it emanated from me. Buster was straining at the end of his lead, his stubby legs attempting to drag me forward as his snub nose snorted and sniffed.

"She's definitely dead, Felicity. I can smell the difference," he informed me. I didn't need his advice on the subject, I could see for myself. I just didn't want to believe it.

"Annabelle?" I called out hopefully. It's nearly Hallowe'en, so maybe this was a trick she had chosen to play on whoever next walked through the door. Or perhaps she was practicing for the night, and she

1

fell quickly into character when she heard someone coming through the front of the shop.

These thoughts played through my head even though I knew they couldn't be true.

"Annabelle?"

"*Definitely dead,*" Buster remarked for the second time.

I was standing just inside the door of the fitting room at the back of Richards' Designer Gowns, there to discuss one of my latest clients. My visit to Annabelle's shop was nothing unusual – her place is walking distance from mine located at the other end of Rochester High Street.

I could have phoned her just as easily, but going to her shop allows me to see the gowns, gets me away from my desk and the infernal computer, and Buster needed a walk.

My name is Felicity Philips. I'm THE wedding planner. If you are wondering about the need for capitals, then I can easily explain. There are lots of wedding planners. When a couple wants to celebrate their nuptials in style and need a person to wrestle all the different elements together then they hire someone like me.

Except they don't hire me because my price tag is too high for them. If you are Rod Stewart or Tom Cruise you hire me. If you are Lord or Lady somebody, then you hire me. If that sounds snobbish, then I beg that you please consider, there are those with an abundance of money and a desire for something above and beyond that which ordinary wedding planners can achieve.

I am THE wedding planner.

That was very well and good, but right now I was trying hard not to hyperventilate, and my feet wouldn't seem to move.

"Annabelle?" I tried for a third time.

Buster stopped sniffing the air and eased off the tension in his lead as he twisted his head around to look up at me.

"*Seriously?*" he asked.

I glanced down, my eyes taking in his expression before flicking back up to once again take in the terrible sight that dominated the fitting room. Annabelle was a yard in front of the counter set at the back of the room, wearing one of her wedding dresses ...

My brain froze.

"Not the Kipling." The words left my mouth without me thinking what I was saying. I was already panting, struggling to get my breath as the horror of finding Annabelle in this state played havoc with my adrenal gland. Now that I could see what dress she was wearing, the horror doubled.

I don't want to be overly materialistic, but in the world of wedding dresses, there is very little that tops a Kipling Original. Annabelle had been lucky in getting this one, the famous designer letting her have it as part of a promotional marketing venture. He was looking to catch the eye of a royal bride.

As it happened, we had a meeting scheduled for later this afternoon because he saw me as a front contender to plan the forthcoming, though not officially announced, royal wedding. If I won the contract, I would suddenly have a lot of very good friends appearing out of the woodwork as they all vied to have me employ them for whatever element was their speciality.

It would be an enviable position to be in if I was able to pull it off.

All this flashed through my head as I stared at the dress. Annabelle's bare arms and legs dangled from it limply. Keeping her aloft was the stand and pole from a mannequin though the torso of the dressmaker's dummy was nowhere to be seen. Around her neck a crudely twisted piece of lace suggested she had been strangled. Or was garrotted the right term, my brain idly questioned.

Taking a breath to steady myself, I looked around for somewhere to secure Buster.

"*Whatcha doing?*" He wanted to know, leaning away from me as I attempted to haul him back to the door.

"I'm just putting you over here by the door, Buster, dear." I had to tug the stubborn little brute quite hard to get him to move. Though he weighs considerably less than me, all his weight and his centre of gravity are roughly in line with my ankles. He was digging his claws in and dragging his bottom on the floor.

"*This situation calls for devil dog!*" he barked at me. "*There's been a murder, Felicity. That means it's action time! If you tie me up, I can't be ready to defend you. What if the killer is still here?*"

At no point had I given any consideration to where the killer might be, so Buster's words instantaneous-ly rooted me to the spot. I had been about to loop the open end of his lead over the hook on which a fire extinguisher hung by the door. Now I wasn't so sure I wanted to.

I needed to call the police. I needed to call for help. But first, I needed to check if Annabelle truly was beyond saving.

Changing my mind about what it was I wanted Buster to do, I dropped his lead and grabbed his back end. It took some effort, but I swivelled his hips around, so he was facing into the room. He couldn't go anywhere, because I was blocking him.

"I need to check Annabelle. Stay here by the door, Buster. There's a good dog. Can you do that for Felicity?"

"Good thinking, Felicity. Leave me at the door to watch your back. If someone comes in, I'll disable them."

I blinked a couple of times. "No, Buster, that's not what I meant at all."

"Right gotcha. You want me here so I can get a run up should the killer come in from the other side."

Here's a thing about my bulldog. He thinks he's a superhero. Or, more accurately I think, he enjoys pretending to be a superhero. He talks and acts as if he is wearing a mask and cape that no one else can see and as if he has ninja skills or something. He has in the past asked me for a collar that would double as a utility belt into which he could put throwing stars and other weapons. If you are wondering how it is that I'm able to converse with my dog, I'm afraid I don't have much of an answer for you.

I can hear my cat, Amber, too. I don't know why or how, but it is just those two animals who share my home. I started hearing their voices just a short while after they moved in with me, obtaining them both from an animal rescue shelter a few weeks after my husband died. They can understand what I am saying and in turn their thoughts and the sounds they make arrive in my head as fully formed sentences. It's all a little bizarre, but one learns to live with it. To my knowledge I'm the only person on the planet who can do this. However, I like to think that is not the case.

Giving up on the task of trying to get the bulldog to just sit and be sensible, I gave him a simple command to stay and then crossed the room to see Annabelle. The faint hope that I might find a pulse was dashed the instant my fingers touched her skin. She was not cold to the touch, but she was not the temperature of a living person either. My brain instantly told me this meant she had not been dead for very long and I gulped loudly enough to hear it myself.

"Oh, Annabelle," I murmured.

Speaking from right next to my feet and making me jump with his unexpected closeness, Buster said, "*See? definitely dead.*"

Tutting, I picked up his lead and led him back to the corner of the room, saying, "I thought we agreed you're going to stay by the door?"

Buster looked at me like I was behaving strangely, a curious expression acted out by his eyebrows.

"*I did stay by the door. I stayed there until you were right next to the body. You didn't specify how long you wanted me to stay there for.*"

I rolled my eyes and muttered a few words under my breath. Like most other days, I could not decide whether the ability to communicate with my pets was a gift or a curse. Now that I had Buster away from the body - I doubted his proximity was going to help the police gather evidence and such - I reached into my handbag to find my phone.

The inside pocket where it always sits was empty. I hauled the bag around to my front, holding it open with one hand so I could root around with the other. It wasn't there. With a groan, I realised I had left it on my desk.

Blowing out an annoyed breath, I made my way back to the front of the shop and the counter where I found a landline.

The phone was an old ... strike that, it was an ancient piece of machinery, fitted with a fax machine – when did you last use one of those? – and a tape recorder for messages. On the front was a large, red liquid crystal clock displaying the time: 1227.

Reaching out to pick it up, the rotten thing rang and scared the living holy heck out of me.

I squealed and almost collapsed as my heart, still beating too fast from the shock of finding Annabelle, now opted to stop altogether.

The phone continued to ring as I found something to lean against, sparkly lights dancing in front of my eyes as I held my chest and tried to decide whether to just die or not.

There was a click and the tape recorder kicked in.

"Annabelle, this is Rudyard. Sorry, I'm having to shout," he shouted. "I'm at King's Cross in London. I know I'm late for my meeting with you. I need to call Felicity Philips for that matter because I'm supposed to be seeing her after I've come to your place. It looks like I'll have to scrub both meetings."

Echoing loudly in the background, the public address system at the station drowned out his voice for a moment.

"Passenger Karen Woodruff please report to lost and found. That's passenger Karen Woodruff to lost and found."

When the announcement ended, I was once again able to make out what Rudyard was saying. "... terribly late. Please accept my apologies. I lost track of time and was late leaving. Call me back and we can rearrange.

Another announcement cut him off. *"The 1227 service to Newcastle is about to leave from platform two. Final boarding."*

Should I answer the phone? He said he was going to call me next, and he wouldn't get me either. What would I say if I picked up the phone though?

"Goodness, it's noisy here," Rudyard complained when the announcer stopped speaking. "Look I've got to go. Call me back."

The line went dead while I was still trying to figure out if I should answer it. On unsteady legs, I picked up the handset and called the police.

Just a couple of minutes later they were on their way to me, and I drifted to the front door to wait for their arrival.

Given a little time to kill, my brain began working overtime. Who could have done this to Annabelle? Why would they want to? Annabelle Richards, an unmarried woman in her late thirties, sold wedding dresses for a living. She did alterations and fittings, making a handsome salary from a single shop in Rochester High Street. I had been sending my brides to her for more than ten years, secure in the knowledge that each one would receive exactly the sort of premier treatment I demanded.

The door bumped against my bottom when somebody outside attempted to come in. I moved forward, expecting to turn and find a couple of uniformed officers. Instead, looking in at me was the face of Annabelle's assistant, Clara.

I stepped back to let her in, then thought better of it, but had given her too much space and she was coming through the door. The fitting room, and indeed Anabelle's limp body, were visible from the front door if one looked through the shop. I could have closed the door leading through, but hadn't thought to do so.

Clara did not need to see her boss in this condition. However, she had seen me through the glass of the door and was already speaking, bustling into the premises with her arms full of bags.

"Good morning, Mrs Philips. I'll be with you in just a second. I just need to put these things down. I expect Annabelle is out the back somewhere."

Buster was getting in my way, trying to come around me to get to the young woman because she always made a fuss of him. Nevertheless, I positioned my-self to block her entry, stopping her from taking another step by filling the doorway.

Unfortunately, I'm only a shade over five feet tall and Clara is about five feet and ten inches. Con-sequently, despite my attempts to prevent it, she spotted Annabelle.

I managed to say, "Clara, I..." before she filled the air with an ear-splitting scream.

She backed away a pace, her eyes widening and her mouth opening. The door was still open, her scream echoing along the ancient buildings of Rochester High Street, and passers-by immediately stopped to look in our direction.

"You killed her!" Clara shouted at the top of her lungs, dropping the bags she held. Sequins and lengths of lace frill spilled onto the floor by her feet although she seemed not to notice. Still backing away, her hands came up to her face. "You killed her!" she yelled again.

Then, turning away to look at the people who were now paused in the street to see the drama unfolding, she jabbed an accusing finger in my direction and yelled once more, "She killed her! She killed Annabelle!"

Dangerous Woman

The sound of distant sirens punctuated the air, as all around me faces turned my way. Suspicious eyes abounded, the citizens of Rochester immediately assuming they were indeed looking at a murderer.

Clara was continuing to back away, one arm still spearing the air to leave no doubt about who she was accusing.

Finding my voice, I said, "I didn't kill her, Clara. I walked into the shop and found her like that."

"A likely story," remarked a man in his fifties as he detached himself from his wife and began stalking toward me. He had an unfriendly face with a bushy beard that sat beneath a completely bald head.

He wasn't the only one coming my way, there were others too, almost exclusively male and all acting brave in front of the audience now forming.

"Don't try to escape now," warned the man with the bushy beard.

"Grab her, Barry!" shouted a woman though I didn't see who it was.

Becoming exasperated by this unexpected turn of events, I responded by saying, "I'm not trying to escape. I haven't done anything to cause me to want to escape. As you can see, my feet haven't moved."

Clara shouted, "Careful! I think she might be armed!"

The person closest to me now was the man with the bushy beard. The woman who had shouted for him to grab me, turned out to be his wife/partner for her next instruction was, "Be careful, Barry!"

Made suddenly wary by Clara's remark, Barry paused in his advance, looking me up and down for any sign that I might have something deadly hidden about my person.

Deciding I was bored with all this silliness and one hundred percent unwilling to get grabbed by any-one, I gave a short tug on Buster's lead.

"It's devil dog time. Defend me."

I'll say this for Buster, he might not be particularly athletic, fast, or even awake most of the time, but you would not want him attempting to bite your lower leg.

He surged forward with his back legs, snarling and barking for emphasis. What I heard in my head was a noise I have come to associate with my ridiculous bulldog transforming into superhero mode.

"Dun, dun, DAH!"

It took all my might to keep Buster in check so that he wouldn't actually bite someone. Beardy Barry was being annoying and aiming his efforts at absolutely the wrong person, but I had to applaud him for his sense of civic responsibility. Getting bitten would be an unfair reward.

Startled by Buster's sudden aggression, Beardy Barry darted back to give me the space I desired.

"She's got a dangerous dog too!" he announced loudly to the crowd.

The crowd was growing, the constant foot traffic through Rochester's High Street never ending at this time of day. With such street theatre playing out, those travelling in either direction were stopping to watch.

Newcomers were asking to be informed as to what was going on and the general consensus of conversation echoing around me was that a crazed killer had just been caught in the act of dispatching her latest victim. The citizens of Rochester were going to ensure I was brought to justice. They could all hear the police sirens approaching and mercifully so could I.

In fact, it was with great relief when the approaching sound abruptly trebled and the white, silver, blue, and day-glow yellow squad car screeched into view at the Chatham end of the High Street.

It's a one-way street if entering from that end, but the police were paying no attention to such restrictions, threading their squad car carefully around the left side of the traffic as they squeezed through by using the pavement.

Still keeping his distance, Barry wasn't above making a snide remark.

"You're for it now," he sneered with a knowing smile.

Buster was keeping full tension on his lead, straining to make sure no one came any closer though his barking and snarling had subsided when they all backed away. Giving his lead another quick tug, I said, "That's enough now, Devil Dog. Thank you for your assistance." I worry that pandering to his fantasy only makes it worse, but he's my doggy and I love him. If pretending to be a superhero makes him happy, then I will support him.

The police had stopped just a few yards away at the edge of the crowd forming around me. Through the press of people, I could see the officers inside getting out, donning their hats as they came, and I noted with enormous relief that I recognised them.

Not that I spend a lot of my time in the company of police officers, you understand. However, there have been a couple of recent occasions where I have come across members of the local constabulary.

I made the mistake of waiting patiently for them to approach, allowing Beardy Barry to get in first.

Without taking his eyes from me, he turned his head slightly to call over his shoulder.

"I've got her here. I performed a citizen's arrest for you, officers."

"No, you didn't," I argued instinctively.

Ignoring me completely, Barry continued, "She's been resisting. That dog of hers is clearly dangerous. Typical for a criminal, having a brute of a dog like that. Horrible mongrel."

I wanted to reply with a cutting remark of my own, but Buster had heard what Barry said and thought it a good idea to respond for himself.

"Mongrel? I'm a pedigree!" he snarled, thrusting forward with all four paws.

It felt like he almost snapped my arm this time when he lunged to snap at Barry's leg, and I'll admit I gave Buster a little more lead than I had been.

I'm sure it was the wrong thing to do, but it did at least create an entertaining comedy moment when Barry backpedalled faster than his legs could manage, slipped on a cobble, and fell neatly on his rump.

As Barry filled the street with some particularly blue language, the two uniformed police officers pushed their way through the crowd.

"I think that's quite enough now, Sir, don't you?" remarked Constable Hardacre. "There are ladies and children present."

A yard behind him, and making a bigger hole as she pushed through the crowd - her attitude demanded it - Constable Patience Woods added her thoughts

"Yeah, shut it, Beardy."

I was facing Constable Brad Hardacre so got to see it when he rolled his eyes, sighed, and shook his head. He made no comment about his partner's choice of words, instead focusing on the task in hand.

"Okay, everyone, settle down now please." Constable Hardacre spoke while turning in a slow circle to meet as many eyes as possible. There had to be more than fifty onlookers now, too curious about what was happening to go about their business. They would be dispersed soon enough, I was sure. Reinforcements were on their way; sirens continued to echo through the buildings, the report of a murder demanding the presence of more than one squad car

As some people began to drift away from the back of the crowd, the constables turned their attention to me.

"I believe you placed the call, Mrs Philips. Is that correct?" asked Constable Hardacre.

Just getting off the ground and dusting off his backside, Barry said, "What?"

Paying no attention to anyone, Constable Woods was crouching to make a fuss of Buster and scratching the fur under his chin to send his back left leg into spasm. She'd first met my dog at the home of Derek and Joanne Bleakwith several weeks ago and he sure remembered her.

With a weary sigh, and an exhalation of exasperated air, I ignored Buster's happy noises and Barry's questions so I could say, "Yes. That was me. Thank you for coming so swiftly."

Now that the police were here, Clara was willing to come a little closer. I thought I was going to have to argue with her, expecting Annabelle's assistant to once again claim she saw me do it. However, the shock of seeing her murdered boss had subsided enough for her brain to filter the facts a little more clearly.

"Sorry, Mrs Philips," she apologised. "You really found her like that, didn't you?"

I nodded. "Of course."

Constable Hardacre said, "Show me."

The next ten minutes were swiftly absorbed as more and more police officers arrived. Some set up a cordon outside the shop and closed the shutters on the windows so that no one could see in. Clara was taken to a back room – not the fitting room where Annabelle still hung. Someone - probably Constable Woods - was making tea.

Patience didn't end up on tea duty because she's a female police officer in an environment still dominated by men, but because she volunteered. I wouldn't say that I know her, but I get the impression she snagged the job because she was hoping there would be cookies.

I guessed right if the evidence was anything to go by. When she brought me a steaming mug of tea some minutes later, there were sugary crumbs on her lapels.

With the scene secured by the constables, the detectives took over, but even with them controlling the scene, they all stopped when a new figure arrived.

Blowing on my hot tea to cool it, I twisted my head around to track several pairs of eyes when urgent whispers encouraged everyone to look busy.

Someone hissed, "Look out lads, God's here."

Coming through the door with an air of absolute authority, strode Chief Inspector Ian Quinn.

One look at me was all it took for his lips to tighten into a thin line of disapproval.

"Mrs Philips."

"Chief Inspector."

Acknowledgements complete, he moved on, guided through the shop and into the dress-fitting room in the back by one of his detectives. There he would find Annabelle just as I had.

Twenty minutes later, I was still waiting for someone to tell me I was free to go and beginning to get a little uppity about being detained. I had found the body, and I knew they would want a statement, but beyond walking into the shop and being bold enough or familiar enough with the proprietor, to wander through to her back rooms to find her, I knew nothing.

I hadn't seen anyone. I hadn't heard anything, and I didn't know Annabelle well enough to have any idea why someone would want to kill her.

Another ten minutes ticked by, and finally Chief Inspector Quinn came looking for me. He didn't approach me though. Rude as he is, he crooked a finger in my direction and vanished back the way he had come.

"You'd better go, missus," opined the constable standing sentry at the shop's entrance. "The chief inspector doesn't like to be kept waiting."

"I couldn't give a stuff what he does or does not like," I snapped smartly. "If he wishes for me to join him, he can jolly well ask politely."

The constable flared his eyes – my attitude unexpected. I couldn't imagine why. Who did Quinn think he was to summon me like a dog? I wouldn't do the same to a dog.

Perhaps he overheard my remark. Perhaps he realised I didn't work for him, but from the back room the chief inspector's voice rang out.

"Mrs Philips, if it pleases you, I have something I would like you to look at."

That was more like it.

JUST LIKE TEMPEST MICHAELS

I held out Buster's lead for the constable to hold. Buster was sound asleep, snoring loudly and probably responsible for the suspicious smell I detected a few minutes ago. It was either my dog or the constable had gastric troubles.

"Could you just hold this for a moment, please?" I begged, demonstrating what manners were supposed to sound like.

Startled into motion, the man accepted the lead, and I went looking for his boss.

The sight of Annabelle caught my breath again, causing me to gasp quietly. One of the forensic chaps, a man in his late forties, was holding her head up and pulling her hair to one side to get a better look at her neck.

"Not your first body, eh?" Quinn remarked. "Can you tell us what you make of the bruising to the victim's neck, Mrs Philips? Why do you think the killer used a piece of material and not their hands to strangle Miss Richards?"

I snorted a hard breath, my heart beating at twice its usual speed.

"Why do you want me to look at it?" I stammered, trying to get my breathing under control. "Annabelle was a friend of mine. Anyway, how would I have the faintest idea why the killer would do anything?" I was beginning to feel dizzy again and wondered if I looked pale because I certainly felt it.

One of the men in suits – the detectives, I assumed – gave his boss a worried look.

"Sir, do you think perhaps we should ..." His words trailed off when Quinn looked his way.

"Yes, Mrs Philips, your friend, who you reported dead mere moments before you were discovered on the premises by her assistant. Can I see your hands, Mrs Philips?"

"My hands?" I repeated his request, not understanding it at all.

He stepped forward, coming into my personal space.

"Yes, Mrs Philips. Your hands."

Confused, and a little overwhelmed by my emotions, I lifted my hands. They had been clasped in front of me, my arms resting against my body, but once I started to move them, the chief inspector grabbed them.

Gripping each wrist hard, he lifted them to chest height, turning my arms over by applying his superior strength.

I protested, yanking my arms to get away from him though his grip proved too strong.

"Hey!"

"Chief Inspector?" questioned the same besuited detective who had spoken previously, this time the timbre of his voice making it sound like he was less likely to back down.

"There's a cut on her hand," he stated, looking across the room at the officers assembled there. "Right where the lace would have cut in."

"Sir?" the detective warned.

One of the forensic chaps, easy to distinguish from everyone else with his full-body, white plastic suit, peered over Quinn's arms to stare at my hands. They were staring at a mark where I had cut myself on the edge of a tin of tomatoes yesterday. I'm still not sure how I did it, but as they focused on my left hand, Quinn's grip on my right fell away.

I reclaimed it, and in a fit of outrage aimed a slap at the chief inspector's right cheek. It resounded around the room like a whipcrack, the room silenced instantly.

Behind me someone whispered, "Just like Tempest Michaels."

I had no idea who that was, but I was seething, my eyes locked on the chief inspector's when he shot me a glare with angry eyes.

"You deserved that, Sir," snapped the detective, venom in his tone. He stepped between us, using an arm to steer me back through the building to the display room at the front.

Leaving the room, I heard the forensic chap say, "Not a match, sir. That's not a fresh wound."

I felt faint from the rush of adrenalin. Had I gone mad? What was I thinking? I had just struck a police officer. A senior one at that, not that I felt rank should make a difference. I was about to question when I had last slapped someone when I realised the answer was just a couple of nights ago.

It happened on a date with Vincent Slater, a local private investigator who had saved my life and made me feel very much in his debt. However, he was just a little too handsy and I clipped him across his cheek. That was just a couple of days ago.

To be fair to Vince, all he did was pat my rump, and I reacted mostly out of surprise, rather than horror or disgust. We had been on several dates, with the unspoken suggestion that it might progress from there one day. I was keeping him at arm's length because I wasn't ready for ... anything. I am a widow and had not expected to ever meet anyone again.

With my work taking up so much time, I hadn't given the prospect of a future relationship a lot of thought. I was still sort of married to Archie in my head even though he had been gone for two years. But then Vince came along, and he was ... well, he was annoying mostly. However, there was a certain charm beneath the rough exterior, and he was very clear that I was exactly what he wanted. He conned me into the first date a few weeks ago where we both got arrested. Then he leveraged another date when he almost died to ensure I didn't.

Back in the display room at the front of Annabelle's shop, I was dragged away from thoughts of Vince and where he and I now stood after I huffily got back in my car and drove off two nights ago, by the detective asking if I would like a glass of water.

"Hmmm?" I replied, only half hearing him. "Sorry, yes, water. Um, no thank you. Was I out of order just then?" I pestered him to tell me.

He shook his head. "Not even slightly. The chief inspector holds a grudge like no man I ever met. He still feels that you got away with murder a few weeks ago."

"But they caught the killer!" I protested.

The detective nodded to the constable standing at the door still holding Buster's lead. My dog hadn't twitched while I was absent. The lead was passed back, and a chair fetched from across the room.

As the constable fell back into his original position, the detective fetched a second chair and settled onto it, sitting adjacent from me, and taking care not to pinch Buster's paw when he set it down.

"I'm DS Wishaw," he introduced himself, then dropped his voice to a lower volume so Quinn wouldn't hear what he had to say. "It ought not to be Chief Inspector Quinn here today; he's not a detective. Unfortunately, my boss, DCI Gower, is cruising toward retirement and currently on gardening leave. Quinn likes to be involved in any case that will make a headline and get him noticed. The moment he heard your name, he started moving and told everyone he was taking over." Speaking at a normal volume again, he said "The chief inspector was checking your hands, Mrs Philips, hoping you would have marks on them from using the lace to strangle the victim."

"Annabelle." I hadn't intended to correct him, it just slipped out.

He accepted it with an apology. "Did you know her well?"

"Not really." I explained our relationship, stating that I had known her a long time, but that we had never seen each other socially. I knew she was single and childless, but whether she had a boyfriend I could not speculate.

When I finished, I said, "Annabelle's clothes were missing."

"I guess the killer caught her by surprise while she was getting changed into that dress."

I jerked, confused by his assumption for a moment.

"No, she wouldn't have been putting that dress on. Is that what you think?"

"Why else would she be wearing it?"

"No reason. Annabelle would have put the dress on the mannequin, but never on herself." I was struggling to figure out how they could be so blind. "Was she, um. Did the killer do anything other than kill her?" I was trying to ask if she was naked beneath the dress because the killer had other intentions, but was having trouble saying the words.

The detective's eyes flared a little as he attempted to decipher my oddly worded question. I saw his features change when he got it.

"No, Mrs Philips. There is no sign that the killer did anything other than strangle her."

"Then she was staged," I stated.

Chief Inspector Quinn's voice echoed from the back room before he appeared moments later. "Yes.

That's obvious, Wishaw." DS Wishaw narrowed his eyes, but refrained from offering a retort. "The killer is most likely a disgruntled bride," he added, making his way through to the front of the building.

"Wait, what?" I sent brides here all the time. I didn't need them to be getting hassled by CI Quinn, the utter pig. "Isn't that kind of a big leap?"

Quinn shrugged. "I've been in this game a long time, Mrs Philips." He reached up to pat his rank insignia. "And I'm good at it. One develops a nose. I saw how thin the waist on that wedding dress is …"

"Obviously. It's a Kipling," I replied. Dresses like that, especially ones made to be in glossy magazines, were always made at size zero. You either dieted to get in them, or you didn't put them on. I couldn't say I like how some elements of the wedding industry operate and think, but it wasn't a battle I fancied taking on by myself.

I got a sardonic smile from the chief inspector. "There will be a fat bride at the root of this, mark my words."

Unable to believe my ears, I was about to rise to my feet. I wasn't sure what was going to come out of my mouth, but since I appeared to have gotten away with slapping his face, I was going to push my luck.

"You can go, Mrs Philips," Quinn cut me off. "You can think yourself lucky I am not pressing assault charges. If you ever attempt to strike me again, I can promise you a stay at her Majesty's pleasure."

It was enough of a threat to shut me up. DS Wishaw was on his feet again, visibly seething. I suspected there was a strongly worded discussion brewing and I needed to be no part of it. The constable opened the door, I dipped my head toward DS Wishaw, wishing him luck as much as anything, and left Annabelle's shop for what I assumed would be the last time.

I was heading back to my own boutique/office. It sat at the other end of the High Street, near the bridge where I enjoyed continual passing traffic. I needed to stop off for coffee, something I promised I would return with, but I only got about halfway along the mile of High Street before I was stopped again.

'Orrible Henri

I live in a nice quiet village where one might rea-
sonably expect to enjoy relatively uninterrupted
peace and quiet. It's not without crime, obviously,
but with the exception of a few burglaries over the
years, there is little to report.

Rochester is a city, but only by definition, by which I
mean it is not the sort of place one usually associates
with the word. Some of the buildings in the High
Street date back to the 14th Century and there are no
big franchises taking over with their giant shops and
massive discounts. Rochester's central business dis-
trict is filled with small eateries and family-owned
shops, some of which can trace their management
back to a great, great, great goodness knows how

many times grandfather who started the business in 1653 or whatever.

Crime here is more likely than where I choose to live, but nevertheless, walking through the High Street in the middle of the day, I do not expect to find my way blocked by a gang of aggressive men.

They stepped out in front of me as I drew level with one of the many small alleyways one finds running between the shops.

Startled initially, the anger CI Quinn had brought to the surface returned the moment my eyes were able to focus on the central figure barring my way. I don't know whether they just didn't see Buster, or perhaps thought he looked docile, but they all jumped back when he lunged for them.

Buster barked, *"I'll kill you all! The night fears me and so should you."*

Momentarily taken aback, Henri swiftly recovered, sneering confidently, "You need to fire him."

I recently took on a new member of staff even though I didn't need one. A young man called Philippe Redmond helped me out in a time of need only to find himself threatened with the sack. To be fair, he had already decided to play hooky from his work because he was upset with his boss. He and Henri were lovers, and Philippe took umbrage when Henri chose to spend the night with his husband instead.

I know, I struggle to bend my head around it too. Regardless, I opened my stupid mouth and hired him on the spot, failing to think through the ramifications. I could find work for him – he was a makeup artist by trade, and a good one at that, but was happy to do anything. The bigger problem was Henri refusing to accept the snub.

"What if I don't?" I challenged. This was not normal behaviour for me, but Buster was going to tear up some trouser legs if I let him go, there were people in the street all around us, and the full head of steam CI Quinn stoked me to was yet to dissipate.

"It could be bad for business," Henri threatened. "That lovely boutique of yours could have all kinds of nasty things happen to it."

Henri had three lieutenants with him, the same three I saw him with at the wedding exhibition a week and a half ago. They were all making each other feel brave; that's what I was telling myself. I was outnumbered four to one, but the thing is, they didn't look like particularly tough men.

Don't get me wrong, they were all taller, broader, and stronger than me. I weigh a hundred pounds on a good day, but they were also wearing more make-up than me, the base layer of foundation making their features look so flawless I had to wonder if they got their chins waxed somewhere.

Breaking the spell, and as if they might have re-hearsed it, the one of the far left said, "Yeah. It might accidentally catch fire."

"Try employing people when you haven't got a bou-tique," sneered the one next to him.

I wanted to point out that the boutique was really just a storefront. Most of my business is conducted over the phone or in client's houses.

I didn't get to though because Henri, next in line and looking like he had something to say, suddenly wasn't there anymore. One second, he was grimac-ing in my direction, trying to look mean, but mostly making me question if he had gas and was trying to hold it in, and the next there was sky where his head had been.

His friends were turning inward on both sides, con-fused about his sudden disappearing act, but they should have been spinning around to face away from me for that was where the danger was coming from.

My niece Mindy was charging toward them, running hard in a fitted dress she had hitched up around her muscular thighs. Henri was on the ground, groaning and clutching his skull where a rock had struck it. The rock was lying a foot away, guiltily looking for somewhere else to be.

I had about two seconds before Mindy went full berserk karate beast on the remaining three makeup artists and I had to move fast to stop her.

"No, Mindy!" I darted through the gap left by Henri, stepping over him to get in her way. I had my arms up and out to the sides, making it all but impossible for her to attack anyone.

The police, a whole bunch of them, were half a mile behind me back at Annabelle's shop. If they heard the shouts and came running ... well, let's just say I'd had enough fun for one day, thank you. Thanks to my swift response, I was fast enough to stop the carnage.

Or so I thought.

My niece, Mindy skidded to a stop, confusion ruling her features with a tinge of disappointment due to her love for hitting people. I forgot one small factor though.

Unsure what his role was now that Mindy was attacking, Buster chose to play it safe and bite someone before I could tell him he wasn't allowed to.

The man to my far left let out a howl, grabbing the man next to him in a frantic bid to stay upright. Buster, essentially a lump of vaguely dog-shaped clay the size of a large footstool, anchored his paws and shook his head.

Buster's victim was already screaming in a convincing falsetto yet managed to add an impressive vibrato right before he lost his battle to stay upright. When he went, he pulled his colleague to the cobbles with him.

"Damn right!" barked Buster, spitting out the man's leg. *"Mess with the bull and you get the dog!"* I wasn't going to bother correcting him.

In what felt like the blink of an eye, the four men facing me had been reduced to one.

He looked about nervously. Just like when Clara shouted blue murder outside Annabelle's dress shop. The people strolling through Rochester High

Street were grinding to a halt, curious to see what drama might be unfolding.

Mindy had her fists cocked – a classic fighting pose – her attention solely on the one man left standing. With her dress hitched up so it barely covered the essentials, and a trio of grown men lying at her feet, it must have looked like a scene from an action movie to the casual passer-by.

The man was backing away, clearly unwilling to join his friends on the ground.

I grabbed her elbow.

"Come on, Mindy," I hissed, tugging her away. "We need to go. Right now!"

"This isn't over," rasped Henri, still on the cobbles and holding his injured head though he was beginning to get up. "This isn't over by a long shot."

Buster asked a question only I heard, and a small snort escaped my nose when I nodded in his direction.

"Go ahead."

Mindy spat a laugh, choking on her next breath as my bulldog lifted his leg on Henri's hip.

I'm a high-end wedding planner. How is it that I have days like these?

Hurrying away, Buster complaining he still needed to go some more, Henri screaming threats at my back, and Mindy performing hand gestures a young lady of nineteen ought to not know, I thought to question how it was she even came to be so far from the office.

"I came looking for you, Auntie," she explained as if it ought to be obvious. "You asked me to speak to those guys from Blue Moon when I was finished organising the catering for Baron Hatley's wedding? Well, I did, and they said they could come now if we were ready. I could have phoned you, but I was halfway to the dress shop already and there is that bakery next door to it ..."

I guess that made sense.

"Then I saw 'orrible Henri," she tortured the word deliberately, "and stopped to watch what he was doing for a second. Next thing I knew, you were there, and he was getting in your face. Is he planning to make trouble because of Philippe? You can't let Philippe know, Auntie. He'll be ever so upset."

"Yes, yes," I dismissed the line of conversation quickly. "You say the paranormal investigators are coming now?"

"If we want them to. I told them where I was going and said I would drop by the office with an answer on my way back."

I was entirely dubious about hiring people who made a living out of investigating the supernatural. Surely, they had to be con men? However, I had walked past their office specifically to take a look, and not only was the premises plush and occupying a prime spot not far from the cathedral, but also the people inside looked tidy and respectable.

Under any other circumstances, I would never entertain the idea of hiring such a firm, but I had a spooky problem and wanted it solved. I was telling myself that there would be a rational explanation for the eerie moaning sound and disturbing voices I'd heard several times now. However, I didn't know what that rational explanation might be, and it was only me who had ever heard it.

What sounded like the quiet, moaning breath of a child in torment wanted me to get out of the premises. That's what it said to me the very first time I heard it. I was at the office working late. *Was* being the right word because I *was* in my car about eight seconds later.

I almost went to the Blue Moon office the very next day – it was when I walked by to have a look, but managing to convince myself I must have imagined what I heard, I chickened out.

It didn't happen again for a couple of days. More pointedly, it didn't happen again until I was in the office after hours by myself once more. This time, the voice told me I was desecrating their home with my business, and I would pay if I ever came back.

I worked from home for two days, pretending I was under the weather when I felt absolutely fine. When anger at being scared from my own boutique replaced the fear, I returned. That was this morning, and I knew I needed to have someone address the issue before an evil spirit attempted to drag me to hell or something.

A cold shiver ran down my spine at the memory of the eerie voice.

The office of Blue Moon Investigations was just ahead to my left. Whether I believed in ghosts or not, I was going in.

Paranormal Investigations

C ompeting with my desire to remove the 'ghost' plaguing my office, was the need to find out which of my brides-to-be was about to get Chief Inspector Quinn pointing a finger at them. I sent many of my ladies in Annabelle's direction, but would be able to interrogate my files to know if it was one of them who would be wearing the Kipling dress. Letting the lady in question know in advance she might have uninvited guests in uniform arriving to quiz her was something I considered to be of paramount importance.

Still, the Blue Moon office was on our way back, so stopping in wouldn't delay me for very long.

There was a lady behind a smart reception desk to the left as we walked in. The nameplate on the desk read 'Marjory'.

She looked up as we came in, "Hello, again."

Her comment was aimed at Mindy, not me, who gave the lady a wave, but had already caught the eye of two men who were chatting at the far end of the office. Both held coffee mugs, and the air in the office hung heavy with the aroma of a fresh brew.

Buster was pulling at his lead again, his nose going nuts.

"*There are dogs here,*" he let me know. "*Dachshunds, I think.*"

I had no idea dogs could tell different species just by smell, but the shorter of the two men ahead of me, looked my way and said something I didn't catch. A second later, two dark blurs shot out from a door behind him.

"Ooh, sausage dogs!" exclaimed Mindy.

The dachshunds flew across the short weave, functional carpet, heading directly for Buster whose tail was wiggling around with excitement.

"Hey, guys! I'm Devil Dog, superhero hound and protector of the weak. The night fears me. What's that? Bull and Dozer?"

I glanced down at the three dogs. The dachshunds were facing Buster, all three dog tails whipping back and forth like mad right before they went into a sniffing routine I chose not to watch.

I couldn't get my brain to focus on what Buster was saying as well as the men coming my way, so I did my best to block out my bulldog's daft noises and extended my hand.

"Felicity Philips."

The shorter of the two men took it. "Tempest Michaels. Pleased to meet you. We already met your ... daughter, is it? This is Ben Winters." He indicated the taller man.

"Big Ben," remarked the taller man, his eyes never leaving Mindy.

I started to correct Tempest, "My niece ..." when his name triggered a memory, "wait, you said, Tempest Michaels. I just heard someone else say your name in conjunction with Chief Inspector Quinn."

Tempest's face took on a pained expression, but his tall friend burst into laughter. "That's because he punched him in the face on live TV!"

I had a question on my lips, but now that Ben, or Big Ben, or whatever it was he called himself, had mentioned it, I could recall the clip being played on local news.

Mindy asked, "Didn't you go to jail for that?"

I gasped, "Mindy!" She was embarrassingly rude sometimes.

Tempest laughed it off. "It's quite all right, Mrs Philips. Yes, I enjoyed a period at her majesty's pleasure. It was quite relaxing."

"Apart from the bit with the golem, right?" asked Big Ben.

I remembered reading about that too. I just hadn't realised it was the same chap.

Moving the conversation along, Tempest said, "You have an issue in your place of business, which is just along the road, yes?"

"Correct," I replied.

"Only auntie can hear it," Mindy supplied, making me sound like a whacko.

"I didn't imagine it," I was quick to defend myself.

Tempest simply indicated toward the entrance. "Shall we?"

Buster dug his feet in again.

"I want to stay here," he whined. *"These guys are cool. They've got all these stories about fighting vampires and werewolves and stuff."*

Not wanting to get into a conversation with my dog in front of people, I tried to speak to him as other owners might.

"Come along, Buster. We have to go now. You can see the sausage dogs another time."

Tempest was standing by the door waiting to go out of it, but seeing me attempting to haul Buster across the carpet, he said, "Maybe I should take my two with us."

Buster spun on the spot while the sausages raced to the far end to get their leads. They had to wait for Tempest to get there, but a moment later, we were all going out the door.

Once we were back in the street outside, Tempest started talking again, asking me questions.

"First things first, Mrs Philips ..."

"Call me Felicity, please," I begged. I was possibly just about old enough to be his mother but being addressed so formally all the time was making me feel like a pensioner.

I got a smile from him. "What I need to know, Felicity, is what you hope for me to achieve, and whether you actually believe you have a ghost. No judgement," he added quickly.

I cannot say what it was that I expected, but the image of a paranormal investigator in my head was not the two handsome, well-dressed men I had walking by my side now.

Tempest Michaels – I think he is the owner of the business – was in his mid to late thirties and dressed in smart casual clothes. He was about six feet tall and athletically built with broad shoulders and a narrow waist. His hair was cut short, but far from a crew cut, and he was freshly shaved. Also, his eyes never stopped moving as if he were pumped on caffeine or operating on high alert the whole time.

His colleague, the aptly named Big Ben, had to be on his way to seven feet tall. He carried too much muscle under his shirt to be called athletic. If anything, he looked more like a body builder. He was shockingly good-looking too, like an aftershave model from a billboard.

He seemed more relaxed than Tempest, but both men exuded a vibe that screamed ex-military.

To answer Tempest's question, I said, "I want to know what is going on, please, Tempest. Before this happened, I would have most very definitely stated that I do not believe in ghosts, but I'm struggling to explain what is making the noise and why I am the only one who can hear it."

I chose to leave out the bit about being able to hear my pets and was relieved when Mindy kept quiet too. I hadn't briefed her, and my secret was exactly the sort of thing she would blurt to complete strangers.

Tempest nodded thoughtfully.

"This is the place?" asked Big Ben, pointing to my office.

Mindy said that it was, and he darted forward to get the door, holding it open with chivalrous charm and a flourished arm as we all passed inside.

Tempest muttered something to him that I did not hear and paused outside while he fiddled with something electronic. I couldn't see what it was, but it was the size of house brick and black. There were no markings I could see, nor even a screen.

As I watched, waiting for him to follow me into the building, he gripped something and pulled. A big antenna extended from one corner to a length of about three feet. When he came inside, he placed it just inside the door and was then immediately speaking to me, stealing my chance to ask him what the device was for.

"This is good, Felicity. I have to establish what people believe because there is no such thing as the paranormal ..."

"*That's not what Amber says,*" remarked Buster though I was the only one to hear him.

"... and it's important to make it clear right from the start that there will be a rational, mortal-realm explanation."

Philippe came through from the corridor that led to our restrooms.

"Ooh, a gay wedding! How lovely!" he clapped his hands together. "This is where Philippe will come to the fore, Mrs Philips."

Big Ben and Tempest exchanged glances, the taller man putting his elbow out for Tempest to take.

Tempest slapped it away, a frown on his face.

"Sorry, old boy," he apologised to Philippe. "We are here for something else entirely." He spun around to face me. "Can you show us the source of the moaning sound your niece described. I believe she said it is coming from an upstairs storeroom?"

I started for the stairs. "Yes, from the chimney in particular. There are some children's initials carved into the brickwork inside the flue." I stopped speaking, suddenly unsure why I was bringing up that snippet of detail. I had been about to question whether their names might create a link to their souls or something and could feel heat rising from my cheeks.

Buster was right, Amber did hold the opinion that the supernatural is all real. She talked about shades and spirits and how cats can see them, but most other creatures cannot. Of course, Amber claimed it is because cats are highly sensitive animals not drooling dung piles. The conversation ended at that point, Buster trying to eat her again and Amber slapping his face with a paw.

In what would have originally been the back bedroom, which had a partial view of the castle if one looked left, and the river if one looked right, I pointed to the chimney.

Big Ben grumbled, "Looks a bit small for a real man to get into. Best if you try, Tempest."

The smaller man, who had to weigh about two of me, rolled his eyes while Mindy giggled.

Tempest said, "You can leave us here and get on with your day if you like, Felicity. We need to check a few things out."

That suited me, but I paused before setting off.

"We haven't discussed your fee," I pointed out.

I got another smile. "Yes, about that. I rather think I will do this for free if that's okay for you. I may wish to come to you for advice at a point in the future."

"He's all loved up," commented Big Ben with an air that suggested he strongly disapproved. "He'll be out ring shopping in no time."

"Oh, romance!" exclaimed Philippe, clapping his hands together again. "Us girlz do appreciate a man who will go the extra mile."

He got a raised eyebrow from Big Ben.

Tempest drew in a deep, slow breath, calming himself rather than reacting. "Yes, well, a ceremony may need to be arranged at an unspecified point in the future. I would like to have someone I can call on for advice if you are content with some quid pro quo for my services."

There was something about Tempest Michaels that I liked. He came across as wholesome and good. His colleague not so much. Big Ben seemed more predatory and it kind of made me glad I was probably too old to be considered a meal.

Mindy, on the other hand, was not. Guiding her back toward the stairs (and away from Big Ben) while shooing Philippe in front of us, I said, "That sounds acceptable to me. Good luck."

I was leaving the paranormal investigators to it – I had other tasks requiring my attention. First of which was to figure out which of my brides had bought or reserved the Kipling dress.

SPLIT THREE WAYS

I had to interrogate my information three times and then call Mindy over to read it too. Philippe – still kind of a fifth wheel because I was yet to figure out what to do with him – came with her, both of my assistants looking over my shoulders as they read from the screen.

"Do you see it?'" I quizzed, impatient to prove I wasn't going mad.

Mindy was frowning hard, her forehead bunched to look like a relief map of the Andes.

"That's the same dress, right?"

"It's a Kipling," murmured Philippe with a sense of reverential grace.

He was right; it was a Kipling, and I was impressed that he could tell just by looking. Rudyard Kipling, choosing the name because it was so familiar to the world, had Colin Cock on his birth certificate. I had known him since he was just an apprentice learning the trade.

He was more talented than his employer would acknowledge, forcing the ambitious designer to strike out on his own. His original line of dresses flopped, the reason being that there wasn't a bride on the planet who wanted to buy a dress from a shop that said 'Cock' above the door.

Who are you wearing? "Oh, I'm in a Cock today." It just didn't ring right.

So he changed his name and relaunched the label, this time with glorious success. He bought his old employer's premises after targeted advertising drove him out of business. If that makes him sound ruthless, then he probably is, but no more so in my opinion than most other business owners.

Personally, I had never had any issue with him, and never heard him so much as raise his voice in my presence. Whatever the case, he made high-end dresses that were highly sought after, and Annabelle came to have one due to a confluence of serendipitous events.

Rudyard wanted to do something special to make himself look benevolent – all part of making sure he was among the front runners to clad the bride at the royal wedding – and chose to make one of his amazing dresses available to a lucky bride.

Annabelle just happened to be in his circle when the marketing ploy was being discussed. She got the dress at a significantly marked down (and undisclosed) price and the task of finding a beautiful, and preferably blushing, bride to fit in it.

I believe it stands as testimony to how topsy turvy my life has been in recent weeks that I had no idea if it was one of my brides who was set to wear the dress. It was no surprise that the dress had attracted some attention, but the shocking detail was that Annabelle appeared to have sold it to three different brides, all of them mine.

"How does that happen?" Mindy questioned.

I didn't have an answer for her, but something else was bothering me.

"I saw this dress earlier today ..." My voice trailed off when I realised I was yet to tell Mindy the news.

Seeing the colour drain from my face as the terrible image of Annabelle resurfaced, Mindy asked, "Auntie, what is it?"

I dipped my head, feeling a little queasy for a moment. When I was able to gather myself, I explained what I found when I got to Richards' Designer Gowns. Philippe, who I believe chooses to act over the top as part of his persona, screeched, "Oh, my God!" numerous times.

Mindy was mostly quiet, but when I finished, she pulled out her phone.

"Was Clara okay?" Her fingers were poised to send a message – young people never seem to call anyone.

The truth was that I had given little thought to Annabelle's young assistant. She couldn't be much older than Mindy, and had not only suffered a terrible shock today, but had also lost her job.

Guiltily, I replied, "I don't know."

Surprising me, Mindy put the phone to her ear – she *was* making a call.

I got to hear one side of the conversation as Mindy wandered across the office for a little privacy. I ought not to be listening in, but I was, though with Philippe commenting on the Kipling dress still, I was finding it hard to hear.

"It's pure genius how he employs an invisible empire line to accentuate the hourglass figure. The way he does it, any bride will look two sizes smaller on their big day."

Mindy had just remarked in amazement, and I needed to hear what she was going to say next. Reaching up with both hands, and straining my hearing, I clamped a hand over Philippe's mouth and gripped the back of his skull to keep it in place.

"How could that have happened?" Mindy asked.

It was hard to make out, but I believed I could hear Clara wailing in her grief at the other end.

"Listen, Clara, it's not your fault, okay? You didn't get Annabelle killed. Auntie says Chief Inspector Quinn is an absolute ..."

I choose to sensor the word she claimed I employed to describe the chief inspector, because not only would I never allow such language to leave my mouth, I'm also not even sure what it means.

She twisted to check if I was listening, her cheeks colouring when she saw my disapproving frown.

"Look, Clara, just go home and get some rest, okay? You don't need to put any more thought to it. I'm sure the killer will be caught." She ended the call after another minute of attempting to calm the dressmaker's hysterical assistant.

Turning to find both me and Philippe waiting for her to report, Mindy puffed out her cheeks and made an uncertain face.

"Clara thinks one of the brides did it."

That didn't come as all that much of a shock because she'd been in Quinn's company for the last couple of hours. I was about to point that out when she said something really rather surprising.

"I think she might be right, Auntie." Seeing the incredulous look on my face she explained, "Clara says she didn't realise it was a one-off designer dress that couldn't be repeated. She's blaming herself because she took deposits from three different brides for the same dress."

That at least explained how it happened.

"But surely Annabelle would have seen the error and cleared it up," I questioned. Annabelle was no amateur and mistakes happen.

Mindy shrugged. "Clara said Annabelle tried, but the brides wouldn't have it. They all refused to take the deposit back and insisted whoever else had placed a deposit would have to forfeit instead."

I didn't like the direction this was going and there was still a major question I needed to raise.

"Clara said Annabelle had to come up with a way to end the dispute because she tried to get Mr Kipling to make new ones – boasted even that she had sold it three times, but he refused to make new ones because it was a one-off design." I didn't say it, but I knew Rudyard only ever made one of each of his dresses. "Clara said he even threatened to sue if she attempted to make a similar dress herself – copyright infringement or something."

I closed my eyes as if that would lessen the sting about to come. "What did Annabelle suggest to end the dispute?"

I heard Mindy suck some air through her teeth. "Well, I guess this makes sense because from the picture that dress can't be more than a size zero – I'd never get in it." Mindy wasn't wrong; she was too meaty. "And the brides are all ... well, bigger than that," she concluded delicately. "According to Clara, Annabelle was going to make the dress a size eight – the furthest she felt she could expand it without ruining the whole thing, and the first one to be able to fit into it …"

She didn't need to finish her sentence; we all saw what she was saying.

The brides in question: Mary Challis, Donna Moscovitch, and Gertrude Blithe-Leatham were all normal size women. None of them was bigger than a size ten … well, maybe Gertrude was, but the point is they were just women. The entire bridal industry is set up to deliver the dream of a perfect woman with an hourglass figure and all the dresses in the shop windows meet that almost impossible stereotype.

There were few brides I'd ever met who did not diet before the big day, many buying dresses one or two or even three sizes smaller than they were with the aim of getting into them. It was for this very reason that I had such good relationships with dressmakers like Annabelle. I needed people I could call on a day before the wedding and have alterations done overnight in time for the big day.

"Annabelle set the girls an impossible task and one of them went nuts and killed her." I said the words with my eyes still closed, picturing all three brides in my head and questioning which had the right temperament for murder. The answer was all or none. I just didn't know.

It didn't have to be the bride though, it could so easily be the bride's father, angry with how upset his little girl was ahead of her wedding. In my head each bride was crying about not being able to get down to the right weight.

Or maybe Annabelle had already announced the winner and one of the losing girls was a pound away from her goal weight. Having tortured herself for the last however many weeks to then be denied in the final hour, she went bonkers and killed the dressmaker.

My eyes snapped open.

"We have to get ahead of this," I stated with resolve in my voice.

"*Damn skippy,*" agreed Buster, lifting his head from the carpet. "*What are we talking about?*"

Ignoring him, I said, "I cannot have any more bad publicity. If one of my brides killed Annabelle, we need to find out which it is and distance ourselves from them before the story breaks."

Mindy ran with the premise. "Okay, Auntie, but which one of them is it? Do we just ditch all three?"

I sucked on my teeth. I didn't like that idea at all.

"No, that would be just as bad for business. All three weddings are in the next four weeks. If I drop the innocent ones now, they will flounder and struggle." A grimace crossed my face. "Plus, they will likely call Primrose," I named my chief rival, "and she will be only too happy to muddy my name while mopping up my mess. No, we have to figure out which of them is behind it."

Buster got to his feet.

"It sounds like you humans are in need of some help. Good thing you know a crime-fighting super-sleuth." He gave himself a shake and reached up with a back leg to scratch his ear. He lost balance and fell over before it connected.

It would be funny if he wasn't at least partly right. I probably would use him. He and Amber both because my pets were most useful at overhearing human conversations and spying when people thought they were alone.

The sound of feet on the staircase silenced our conversation. The Blue Moon boys were coming down.

someone's watching

Tempest was in the lead, Big Ben following close behind as they descended the steps to join us. Tempest started talking before he got to the bottom.

"You'll be pleased to know we found your 'ghost'." I was looking at his hands, wondering if, since he stated it would not be a real ghost, he might have a device of some kind in his hands. "We found a tiny, digital one-way radio unit fitted deep inside your chimney. It appears to have been lowered down the flue – it's dangling from a cable. There's a camera too."

"In the chimney?" Philippe questioned.

Tempest raised one eyebrow.

"No, it's across the street on that sign." He swivelled on the balls of his feet to aim an arm across the road. Above head height – unless you are Big Ben, I suppose – something I couldn't recognise as anything was fastened to the galvanised steel pole by a pair of cable ties.

"How on earth did you spot that?" I wanted to know.

Tempest shrugged. "I was looking for it. You described that the 'ghost' only talks when you are here by yourself, so whoever is doing this has to know when that happens. The obvious answer would be one of your staff ..." he was quick to add, "but that seemed unlikely in this case, which led me to look for a camera. It had to be fitted outside since you would notice someone erecting a camera inside your office. Also, it would need to have a decent view of the inside to know who was here and who had gone home for the day. It was easy to spot once I knew what to look for."

"Are they recording us right now?" asked my niece, a fresh supply of steel in her tone.

Tempest shook his head. "No, I'm blocking the signal. That's what the box over there is for. It's an old army device designed to interrupt radio signals. We used to carry them on patrol in places like Iraq or in Northern Ireland to stop people triggering bombs as we went past. Of course that only worked if they were to be triggered by radio."

It was my turn to shake my head, amazed at what these men knew and what they had achieved in a handful of minutes. I made no remark about guessing their backgrounds correctly.

"So what now?" I asked. "We remove the camera and the ... radio thingy, and that's it?"

Tempest turned to face me. "That's down to you, Felicity. We can absolutely do that if you like – no one likes to be spied on. Or Big Ben and I can trace who set this up and turn them over to the police."

This was news. "You can do that?" asked Mindy.

Tempest made a 'maybe' gesture.

"The law on this stuff is a little iffy. We would need to be able to prove they were deliberately spying on you and that they intended harm – either to you or to your business – through the use of their 'ghost'. To get a settlement you would have to pursue them through civil court at your own expense, and there's no guarantee you would win. It's on you to provide the burden of proof."

I'd heard enough and waved him to stop.

"I already know who it is."

Mindy frowned, "You do?"

"It's Primrose. Who else could it be?"

Tempest raised his hand. "Primrose?"

Mindy, Philippe, and I all joined in to regale the Blue Moon chaps with Primrose stories, especially the most recent one from the exhibition in London.

"So she has it in for you," Tempest concluded.

Big Ben asked, "Is she attractive? Because ... you know ... I can make her forget all about her interest in messing with you if you want. No fee whatsoever."

Tempest rolled his eyes again, and though I wasn't sure, I had a sneaking suspicion that his oversized companion was offering to sleep with my rival.

Preventing me from confirming his intentions, Tempest distracted me with a question. "We can do whatever you wish, but my suggestion is to let us figure out for certain who is behind the ruse and then we can confront them. A warning that their activity is criminal – even when it isn't – is usually enough to stop people from misbehaving again."

I could well imagine that a visit from the two imposing men would be enough to steer me away from a course of action. Decision made, I thanked them both and let them go. Tempest promised to return later and took a set of keys in case he needed to access the premises after hours. I got a promise he would speak to me before doing so if indeed he thought it necessary.

He took the radio signal blocking thingy with him and when the office was silent again a moment later, I found my assistant's looking at me.

Mindy spoke first.

"So, Auntie, which of the brides do we start with?"

THE BRIDES

It's worth noting at this point that my record for sleuthing things out and finding the right answer is nil for three. I just don't seem to have the kind of brain that sees around the corners or into the dark places to find the things the killer tried to hide.

I have a friend called Patricia Fisher who can do it. I have seen her in action, watched her captivate a room and make Chief Inspector Quinn look like a petty fool. I can't do that though. Or at least, I haven't had any luck trying to so far.

It was mid-afternoon, and the sun would begin to dip toward the horizon soon. That meant we could only get so much done today before it would get too late to be knocking on doors. Arguably, I ought to be leaving it to the police, but though that might be the sensible choice, I was prepared to stick my nose into their business because nothing could take priority over preventing the impending PR disaster I could see looming on the horizon.

I had to tread carefully though. A bride is a thing to be cherished and worshipped, the big day all about her and no one else. For that reason, if I was going to quiz them to see who might have killed Annabelle, I had to do it surreptitiously.

With that in mind, I didn't want to disturb two of them at all. If I could narrow the three brides down to one probable suspect, I could make sure they were off my books before the arrest was made.

If possible.

Clearing one of the tables set against the back wall, the one on which we keep the cake and venue brochures, I placed three photographs taken from the brides' files. Beside each picture I placed an A4 pad and a pen – a different colour for each bride.

What can I say? I'm an organiser.

Mindy and Philippe came to stand either side of me once they finished carting the brochures to the back bedroom upstairs.

All three of us stared at the pictures and the notepads.

From the side of his mouth, Philippe whispered, "What do we do now, Mrs Philips?"

Damned if I had the first idea.

I scratched my chin and tried to force my brain to come up with something.

"Well, Donna's father looks like a gangster," I remarked, clutching at straws.

"Ooh, that's good." Mindy darted forward to get a pen and wrote 'Gangster dad' on the notepad next to Donna's photo in large letters.

Philippe asked, "How does someone look like a gangster? Does he wear a trilby and spats?"

Mindy gave him a curious look, "What are spats?"

I had to cut Philippe off before he went down a rabbit hole of explanation.

"He has tattoos on his knuckles and on his neck which, by the way, is as thick as a rhino's ankle. He's got money, but doesn't appear to have much of an education. When I showed him the menu for the wedding breakfast, he struggled to read it." I was being highly judgemental and openly critical, two things I constantly tell Mindy off for. We provide a service for the wedding party and their guests. What they get up to, who they are – provided they are not actually criminals – is none of our business and we show them respect at all times.

Mr Moscovitch did look like a gangster though.

"What about Gertrude Blithe-Leatham?" prompted my niece. "I seem to remember her as rather demanding. Her mother too. They wanted everything exactly how they described it."

That was true for about seventy-five percent of all the brides I ever met. And their mothers. Mindy wasn't wrong though.

"Could we phone them?" asked Philippe. "Maybe one of them will sound guilty."

I opened my mouth to say something, but whatever response I might have been about to give died on my lips when the simplicity of his idea struck me. I had a duty to inform all three ladies about the dress, so why not get on with that right now?

Two of them were innocent – I did not for one second believe the brides could have colluded against Annabelle. Beginning to think it through as I headed for my desk to collect my phone, I doubted I could figure out which of them might be guilty just by hearing the timbre of their voices. That thought was then enforced when I remembered we had already considered that the killer could be among the brides' immediate family.

"You're calling them now?" asked Mindy.

I found my phone – it was under a file which was why I failed to spot it wasn't in my handbag before I left to visit Annabelle. Tapping the screen to bring it to life, I spotted the little red icon showing a voicemail message. Normally, I would check such a thing immediately, but I already knew it was from Rudyard and what the content of his message would be having heard it in Annabelle's shop.

Holding the device aloft, I glanced at my niece.

"Shall I call one of them?" she offered.

"I think I need to visit their houses to break the news in person."

"*Road trip!*" barked Buster.

Mindy flicked her eyes from me to the dog and then back to me.

"What did he say?'" she wanted to know.

Philippe shook his head. "I still can't get used to this. I wish I could understand what Buster says."

I chuckled. "Trust me on this, it's more curse than gift and Buster rarely says anything sensible."

Buster stopped panting for a second, twisting his head around to look up at me.

"You know I can hear you, right?"

I reached down to ruffle the fur on his head. "Of course, Devil Dog. I love you very much. Now be a good boy and multiply thirteen by seven for me."

Buster squinted with concentration as he attempted to perform a task that would keep him occupied for so long he would lie down and go to sleep before he worked it out. With my dog suitably distracted, I returned to what I was doing.

"I'll phone them. I have their mobile numbers so will tell them we need to meet today and make it up from there. I'm sure with their weddings this close, they will all be keen to see me today."

Philippe asked, "What are you going to tell them?"

I didn't exactly have a plan. "Something cryptic," I replied, trying to sound like I had a clue what I was doing. "Like, I could say there is an issue with the dress, and we need to discuss it in person. I won't tell them what it is though."

Mindy's eyes flared, her expression concerned.

"Auntie, you do realise that one of the ladies you are about to call is a stone-cold killer who forced Annabelle into a dress and strangled her, or strangled her and then forced her into a dress."

"And then posed her using a mannequin pole," added Philippe, repeating what I had told them.

Mindy said something I hadn't yet considered. "You calling like this will almost certainly tip the killer off."

There was a lull in the conversation, the three of us all looking at each other, a sense of dread creeping over me.

The door opened, the unexpectedness of it making all three humans jump and Buster bark.

"Whoa!" Justin, my master of ceremonies, reacted as if we had hidden behind a corner and all leapt out to startle him. "You scared the bejesus out of me. What's going on?"

I paused my intention to make the first phone call and met Justin's startled eyes with sorrowful ones.

"Annabelle Richards was murdered this morning."

He blinked, looking from me to Mindy and then Philippe.

"You're not joking, are you?"

It would have been a rather sick joke to play on anyone. I didn't answer his question directly, but I did go to him, placing a hand on his shoulder and doing my best to make sure he wasn't too rattled by the news. I had been terribly shocked earlier, only pushing through it at the time because Clara walked in on me, and everything went crazy.

Tonight, I would most likely have time to reflect, and I wasn't looking forward to that.

When Justin asked me to tell him what happened, I did my best to explain the events of the last two hours. Justin listened with grave interest, interrupting only once or twice to ask questions.

When I was finished, he asked, "Which of the brides do you think it could be?"

"That's precisely what I intend to find out." Saying it with grit in my voice, I then thumbed through my contacts list, stopping on the entry for Donna Moscovitch.

She answered almost instantly. "Mrs Philips?"

I did my best to sound upbeat even though I really didn't feel it.

"Hello, Donna. I'm calling to talk to you about your wedding dress."

"Oh, goodness, yes, I'm just about at target weight. It will be such a relief to be able to eat carbs again. Oh," she gasped, "you're not calling to tell me one of the other girls beat me to it, are you?" The concern in her voice came through loud and clear.

"No. No, that's not why I'm calling."

She performed an exaggerated sigh of relief, "Wheeew! You had me worried there for a second." Donna Moscovitch was the middle of three daughters, and as her name suggests her lineage is Russian. Her mother is English. Petite and pretty, Eleanor Moscovitch was one of those people who got looks but not necessarily brains. I guess she didn't need the latter to score a husband with serious money, though as discussed earlier, the source of that money was a little suspect.

Her father barely spoke on any of the three occasions I'd met him so far. He would grunt or nod to give a response to direct questions, but conversation was not a skill he possessed. The few words he did say, all came with a thick Russian accent.

I had to let Donna know about the dress, but I had a vague plan. It was a hopeful, speculative plan, but that didn't mean I couldn't pull it off. It would cost me a favour, but that was okay in this business.

"Donna, I'm very sorry to inform you that Annabelle Richards, the dressmaker who was selling you the dress, died this morning."

I got silence from the other end. It stretched on.

Just before I felt I needed to check if she was still there, she said, "Do I still get the dress?"

Psychologists might have a field day dissecting the sense of self many brides assume in the run up to their weddings. Not just brides, I've seen similar behaviour from mothers and mother-in-laws too. Nothing else matters. There could be a terrorist with a nuclear bomb in the area and they would be asking if the florist had been able to get the exact shade of lily they specified.

To answer, I fixed my voice with the correct tone of sympathy.

"No, Donna. I'm afraid that won't be possible." I didn't tell her Annabelle had been wearing it and was strangled with some spare lace. She didn't need details. Hearing her begin to hyperventilate at the other end, I was quick to add, "All is not lost, Donna. I know the designer personally. He called me on the phone today. I plan to call him and see if it might be possible to have a replacement made"

"A replacement?" she sobbed. "Why would you call me and terrify me like this if you can just get a replacement?"

There were more voices at the other end now, Donna's mother and sisters quacking around her as they tried to find out what had upset her so.

Trying to explain, I said, "Well, because I felt duty bound to let you know the dress is no longer available, and ... well, because I cannot promise to get you a replacement Kipling Original. I will do my best," I hastily added, when I heard her draw in a sharp breath. "I think I can, but until I have it in my hands ..."

Calming slightly, Donna managed to mumble and apology, "I'm sorry. You're right. Thank you for letting me know. Do you really think you can get a replacement Kipling Original? I really wanted to be in a magazine."

I had no idea if Rudyard would make a new one or not, but with the royal wedding looming and his desire to be my friend just in case I got the gig, I figured I could lean on him a little.

With confidence I hoped was justified, I said, "Yes, Donna. I'm fairly sure I can."

We talked for a few moments more, Donna asking me questions about other elements of the wedding – could they go over the seating plan again because her Aunt Misha had annoyed her mum and they needed to shift her to the back of the room. While she did that, I manoeuvred to get in a question I wanted to ask.

No obvious opportunity came up, so I blurted it just before we ended the call.

"Is your father around at the moment?" I knew he travelled for work even though I had no idea what his work entailed. Mob hits was my top guess.

Donna ought to have thought the question was an odd one for me to pose, but if she did, I got an answer anyway.

"No, he's in Prague. He flies back tonight. How soon will you know about the dress, Mrs Philips?"

When I got off the phone, Mindy and Philippe were waiting to hear what I had to say.

"It's not her," I let them know. "And her father is out of the country, so it's not him either."

Mindy grabbed two of the pictures from the table against the wall.

"That leaves Mary and Gertrude. Who do you want to call next?"

It was a toss, up but I picked Mary Challis. With Mary's phone beginning to ring wherever it was, I lifted my device to my ear.

Justin, initially thrown by my revelation, had made himself a coffee, nursing it and standing off to one side during my call to Donna. Now I was making a second call, he moved to his desk, turned on his computer, and was probably about to start doing something when the office main line started to ring.

Typically, Mindy or Philippe would have answered it, but Justin was closer. My phone continued to ring in my ear, Mary at the other end refusing to pick up. When it switched to voice mail a moment later, I had to decide whether to leave a message and what it ought to contain if I did.

I settled for something simple. "Hi Mary, this is Felicity Philips." Justin, who had been talking to someone, started gesticulating to get my attention. "I have an urgent matter about which we need to speak. It is regarding your wedding dress."

With his hand over the speaker bit of the handset, Justin mouthed. "You need to take this."

"Please call me as soon as you get this. It's Felicity," I concluded, thumbing the green button to end the call.

Narrowing my eyes a little as I questioned who might be calling, and worried it might be the police or one of the brides getting in touch because she already knew about the dress ... I gasped. If it was one of the brides – Mary or Gertrude obviously - the only way they could know was if one of them had killed Annabelle! Surely the police hadn't had enough time to investigate the crime and already be knocking on doors. Would they even have figured out who the dress was going to yet? Had Clara told them?

Excited now, and secretly hoping it was Gertrude, because she was bossy and demanding at a bridezilla level, I put my own phone down and hustled across the room.

"Who is it?" I hissed, keeping my voice quiet.

He could have said any name at all, and it would not have surprised me as much as the one that left his lips.

"Patricia Fisher."

"What?" I stared at him in confusion.

Philippe asked, "Who's Patricia Fisher?"

Justin pushed the handset toward me, forcing me to take it.

"She says she needs a wedding planner."

Across the room, Mindy was explaining to Philippe – the only one of us who wasn't at Loxton Hall for that debacle of a weekend almost two months ago now – exactly who Patricia Fisher was and why he ought to have heard of her. A heartbeat later, the young man had his phone in his hands and was undoubtedly looking her up.

My attention wasn't on him though, I was thinking joyous thoughts and grabbing for the phone.

"Patricia, is that you? Did that handsome captain of yours finally pop the question?"

The voice of my old friend came through crisp and clear when she laughed.

"I'm afraid to report that it is not my wedding that caused this call." There was a wistful pause before she added in a thoughtful tone. "I will call upon you if that changes. Right now though, I have a billionaire and his intended looking for someone who can arrange a short notice, but over the top ceremony on board a cruise ship."

"Really?" My reply came across with all the surprise I felt. Not surprise that Patricia had thought of me, but that there was to be a wedding on a cruise ship, and I might have a legitimate reason to travel. I hadn't left the country since my husband died. "Where will the ship be?" This was the piece of information I wanted more than anything else. Somewhere hot, please.

"That depends on how soon you can pull things together."

My conversation was attracting eavesdroppers, Justin, Mindy, and Philippe all hearing me say 'ship' and enquiring about its location. They knew who Patricia was and that she worked on a cruise ship and were bright enough to be putting two and two together.

"The couple are chomping at the bit to make arrangements. We are about to land at the British Union Isles if that helps. For the next week or so, the itinerary has us cruising south to Rio in Brazil, and then swinging north to take in some Caribbean Islands then onto Miami and New York. The groom is American and due to depart the ship in New York. That gives you about three weeks," she said with an apologetic tone. "I know that's not a lot of time ..."

My mind was racing, filling with questions about whether we had the capacity to pull off a miracle.

My team watched as I raced around my desk and plopped into my chair. With a tap of the mouse, the screen of my computer burst into life.

I was yet to reply, causing Patricia to prompt me, "Any thoughts?"

"I'm just checking my diary," I murmured, my attention on the screen as I changed it to show the next four weeks. This weekend was free – I knew that already. Actually, I knew precisely what I was doing every weekend from now until Easter next year, but to figure out if I could squeeze in an extra, unplanned event, I needed to see what else I was set to do. There were venue visits with prospective couples, dress fittings, cake tastings, and all manner of other appointments. My presence at all of them wasn't strictly required, but it had always been my practice to smooth out the creases wherever I could.

I set the phone down and pressed the speaker button. "We have a gap three weekends from now."

"It doesn't have to be a weekend," Patricia replied instantly.

Mindy took a step toward my desk, an excited expression teasing her eyes.

"Wait. Are we doing a wedding on a cruise ship?"

I flicked my eyes up, lifting a hand and extending an index finger to tell her to wait.

Replying to Patricia, I said, "That actually makes things easier." In my head, mental calculations were taking place. Flights across the Atlantic and back would eat up two days, though the return leg would probably be at night. We needed to ... heck we needed to do everything, and it had to happen in the next few days. "Is there a guest list? Can I use the onboard catering? Is there a venue for the wedding breakfast? Have the couple given any thought to what they want? Is the ceremony going to be on the ship or when it comes into port somewhere? Is there someone who can perform the ceremony?"

Patricia's laughter tinkled in my ear. "Goodness, Felicity. That was a lot of questions."

I wasn't even halfway through the list in my head and new questions were joining the back of the queue at an astonishing rate.

"I can schedule another call and have the bride and groom on the line. If you email across a list of questions shortly, I can have them considering their answers in advance. They were talking about their guest list when I last spoke to them – there are a few famous names on it, I can tell you that for free."

This was beginning to sound better and better; I wish I had more friends who would bring me top drawer clients with money to spend in exotic locations. An image of a new branch of the business swam into my head – Felicity Philips Exotic Weddings in the Sun. It had an appealing ring to it.

Shaking my head to shift the fantasy, I came back to reality. With a deep breath, I committed us to what might prove to be our most challenging wedding of the year. It was going to be the fastest that was for sure.

"Okay, Patricia, I'm in. My whole team is." I got a big, excited double thumbs up from Mindy who was flashing a cheesy smile at Philippe. He didn't seem to know quite what was going on, and Justin had an uncertain or unreadable expression. "Thank you for thinking of me."

Patricia laughed again. "How many wedding planners do you think I know? This isn't a done deal though, the couple – Betty Ross and John Oswald – were happy for me to introduce you, but ultimately, the decision comes down to them on whether they hire you."

That was fair enough and not something that concerned me. I snatched a pen to jot their names on a post-it note, continuing to chat with Patricia as I did.

A minute later, we ended the call. There were voices in the background at Patricia's end – that young Californian friend of hers, and her butler with the fake British accent I thought. They were all going ashore and excited about it.

Patricia promised to arrange a call with the prospective clients and the call ended.

Mindy was vibrating with energy and poised to throw questions my way the moment I put the phone down.

"Are we going on a trip, Auntie? Are we? Where are we going? It sounded like you said it was in a couple of weeks. That's right at the start of November? Will it be hot?"

Philippe joined in. "Can I get a winter tan? Is it going to be in America? I though I heard the lady say New York. I've always wanted to go shopping on 5th Avenue."

Justin raised his hand. "I can't go. Not in the next few weeks."

I nodded, accepting his statement. He had young children and one of them – the eldest I felt certain – was about to have a birthday.

To ward off further questions from the younger demographic and to provide a few answers, I said, "We are yet to be awarded the wedding, but yes, there is a chance we will all need to board a plane and meet a giant cruise ship on the other side of the Atlantic."

Mindy punched the air, "Woo-hoo!"

"What are you so excited about?" I questioned. "Your parents take exotic holidays all the time."

She made a scoffing sound. "Ha! They used to. Mum and dad haven't taken a holiday together in two years and dad stays late at work every day recently."

This was news to me.

"Are you saying they are having problems?"

Mindy tilted her head to one side and gave a shrug.

"I think they used to have problems. Now they just don't really talk to each other."

It was sad to hear and more so because I just didn't know. In the office in front of other people was not the right place to discuss the subject, but I was going to have to pin Mindy down and quiz her about it soon. If she was suffering because her parents weren't talking, she had been remarkably quiet about it. My sister and I had never been close and her attitude toward me had gotten worse as my business went from strength to strength. She resented my success, which was ridiculous. She had a child, something I failed to achieve, and to me that far outweighed whatever comfort and joy my business success could bring.

Moving swiftly on, I said, "We need to prepare fast if we are going to squeeze this extra wedding in. We can't do that now though, our efforts need to be all about the three brides and their families because someone from that cast of people killed Annabelle Richards."

My mobile phone rang. I glanced at it, hoping it might be Mary Challis replying to my voicemail message, but the name displayed was Gertrude Blithe-Leatham. Why was she calling at this time? Did she know? How could she possibly unless she was the killer?

Steeling myself, for Miss Blithe-Leatham was something of a handful, I lifted the phone to my ear.

"Gertrude, I'm glad you called."

"My dress," she didn't bother with any niceties. Ever. "What happened to my Kipling dress?"

My eyebrows pinched together and my heart beat faster. "How do you know about the dress, Gertrude? Have the police been to see you?" I posed the questions nonchalantly.

"The police? No. Whyever would the police want to speak to me? I, um ... never mind how I know, Mrs Philips," Gertrude snapped in her usual brash manner. "I want to know why I didn't hear it from you."

I had my hand over the phone as I mouthed to Mindy, "It's Miss Blithe-Leatham. She knows about the dress." The subtext of my statement was clear – she had just moved to the top of our list of suspects.

Taking my hand away from the phone again, I said, "Yes, Gertrude. Please accept my apology. Today has been a little hectic. Please don't fret though, I know Rudyard personally. Can I meet with you to discuss options?"

Without needing to think, she snapped, "Yes. The sooner the better. I want an exact replacement for that dress."

That suited me. Though I suspected her of murder, I was about to leave the office to meet her.

We agreed to meet at her house in forty minutes – she was currently at a spa in West Malling. It left me with a little time to kill before I needed to set off. I was taking Mindy with me, leaving Justin to work on the next wedding on our calendar. It was in just ten days' time.

Philippe, disappointed to be getting left behind, was going to assist Justin and learn from him. There were final arrangements to be made and all that had already been arranged now had to be double and triple checked. Were the flowers ready? Was there any increase or decrease in the cost quoted for the blooms? Had the caterers ordered all the specialist food required for the wedding breakfast?

It was a long list.

We needed to get going, but had just enough time to grab some lunch. I sent Mindy to buy sandwiches. A leisurely bite washed down with a glass of wine in one of Rochester's many eateries sounded nicer, but there was no time for that today.

When Mindy came back through the door a few minutes later, she had a cardboard cup holder loaded with four travel cups dangling from her right hand and a white paper bag in her left.

Quite literally plonking them both down on an empty square of Justin's desk, she called, "Come and get them."

"We're taking ours with us," I told her, spearing my Marc Jacobs coat with one arm, and hooking my handbag once I had the other arm in too. I was rushing, keen to find out if Gertrude might be behind Annabelle's murder before the police had the chance to arrest her.

From the cup carrier I selected the one with an 'F' on the side, took a quick sip to check it was right, and spun off one heel to head for the door.

I froze instantly.

The entrance to my building was filled from one side to the other by an imposing figure in a sharp suit.

RUDYARD KIPLING

I n my head I heard my knuckles crack.

"*Vince!*" barked Buster, his little piggy tail wiggling with excitement. Buster loved Vince. He thought the security specialist/private investigator was not only great but also clearly the perfect man for me.

This was largely because Vince found out about my talking to the animals thing and was smart enough to use it against me. He played up to my cat and dog whenever he got the chance, offering them the choicest treats and it worked like a charm because they were easily swayed.

It was one of the other reasons our dating lasted a few days and never got beyond a meal out. Basically,

I questioned the motives of a man who was prepared to bribe my cat with whole prawns the size of a man's thumb.

Vince pushed the door open and stepped inside, greeting everyone with a big smile.

"Hello, everyone."

Mindy, Philippe, and Justin returned his greeting with the same level of gusto he employed, and Buster was tugging at his lead so hard I had to let him go. I felt a little betrayed. These were my people, and they were supposed to be on my side.

Vince crouched to fuss Buster, the daft bulldog rolling onto his back for tummy tickles. When Vince rose to his full height again, he shot me a wink to match his lecherous grin.

A muscle by my right eye twitched.

Keeping my voice calm, though it came out as a quiet growl, I asked, "What are you doing here, Mr Slater?"

"Mr Slater? That's a little formal, isn't it? I came to help, darling."

"Don't call me that," I warned, aware that my requests to drop the pet names had achieved nothing in the past. It seemed as if his sole purpose in life was to annoy me.

"Of course, Kitten."

The muscle by my eye spasmed again.

"We are just leaving, Mr Slater." I lofted my handbag and coffee to emphasise that he caught me in the act of going out the door.

I got an approving nod. "Off to see one of the brides suspected of Annabelle Richards' murder, yes?"

I gawped, my mouth open. Then the gears in my head aligned and I spun on my heels to face back into the room.

"You called him?" I aimed my accusation at Mindy.

Mindy looked shocked. "I didn't call him," she denied the charge convincingly.

My eyes swung toward Philippe, but he said, "I don't have the gentleman's number."

"No one called me, babe," Vincent remarked. "I just know things."

I spun back around again, thinking I ought to be getting dizzy. I knew I was glaring at him, and as usual, instead of making him cower, the effect was to draw a burst of laughter.

"Okay, okay. I have a chap whose job is to listen to the police band. He knows enough to call me when he hears your name. That's what happened a couple of hours ago. I called a friend of mine who just happens to be a detective sergeant and I got the low-down from him. I figured, given all that has befallen you recently, you would be looking to get ahead of this thing so no mud could come your way. I am here to offer my help as a seasoned professional investigator." He showed me his teeth; a broad and cheery smile stretching across a face I felt like throwing my drink at. "For free, obviously," he added. "It's not like I can charge the love of my life."

I almost crushed my coffee cup.

From between clenched teeth, I ground out, "I. Am. Not. The love of your life!"

Vince lowered his voice to a gentle whisper nothing short of a verbal caress, "But you could be."

Everyone else in the office was keeping quiet, pretending they were busy doing something while unavoidably listening to the idiot private investigator as he tried to wind me up.

I drew in a deep breath, my eyes closed. When I opened them again, Vince was no longer a thing I cared about. That was what I was telling myself, and it was going to take some effort to convince me otherwise.

"Shall we go, Mindy?"

Mindy looked unsure. "Um ... yes?"

"Jolly good." I put my coffee down, checked my handbag again, picked the coffee up once more, and walked around Vince as if he were nothing more than a rock in a stream.

Mindy muttered something I didn't catch as she left the office behind me.

Vince called out, "Right, so I'll just follow you then?"

He did not get an answer.

At my car, a sleek Mercedes SL 500 convertible, I placed the coffee on the folding hard roof for a moment to fish around for my keys.

Forced to wait for me to open the car, Mindy said, "Your relationship with Vince is a little odd, Auntie."

Without looking her way – I'd finally found the keys and was getting in, I remarked, "That's because the only place our relationship exists is in Mr Slater's head."

"He seems very sweet for you though." Mindy commented, the words she employed were drawn out at the end, the nuance making it more of a question than a statement. She was asking why I felt it necessary to keep him at arm's length. "I thought the two of you went on a date."

Mindy slid into the car, Buster bounding in from my side to take up his usual spot in the passenger's footwell.

"Three dates actually. There will not be a fourth."

Mindy thought about that for a moment, before tentatively wording her next question.

"Is there an issue with ... you know, bedroom stuff. Couldn't he ... um. Did he have?"

I was already reeling from the fact that my nineteen-year-old niece was asking me about my sexual habits, but struggling to understand what precisely she was asking me, I got it in vivid colour when she held out her index finger and made it droop.

"WHAT? What on earth?" The car had just started to move forward, and I stepped hard on the brake, jolting us both into our seatbelts. Twisting in my seat, enough heat coming from my cheeks to warm a room in January, I tried hard not to shout. "Mindy, for a start, Mr Slater and I never so much as kissed." She raised her eyebrows like that just didn't sound true. "Secondly, you and I are never having a conversation of this nature again. Okay? Mr Slater and I are not an item and never will be. He has a screw loose in his head, but he will get the message eventually."

Mindy puffed out her cheeks. "If you say so, Auntie."

"I do."

She was quiet until I started driving again. "You know, there's nothing wrong with a little later life romance."

"How would you know?" I was raising my voice again. "You're still a teenager."

"I read," she replied grumpily. "I'm just saying, how many chances does a person get. Vince looks after himself. He has his own money."

"You go out with him then!"

Mindy's face turned itself inside out. "Ewwww, Auntie!"

It was enough to end the conversation, the next twenty minutes spent in relative silence as I wound the car through the Kent countryside.

Halfway to our rendezvous with Gertrude, I remembered I was supposed to have called Rudyard Kipling. Tutting at myself, I pressed a button on the car's central console to activate voice dialling.

"Call Rudyard Kipling," I commanded in a loud, clear voice.

With its electronic voice, my car replied, *"Calling Roger Tipton,"* and proceeded to do precisely that.

Swearing, and taking my eyes from the road, I stabbed the button to end the call. Trying again, I enunciated my words with perfect, clipped English.

"Call Rudyard Kipling."

"Calling Xuan Dynasty Chinese Takeaway."

Mindy stabbed the 'End Call' button this time.

"Good grief, Auntie. I'm sitting right here." Calmly she selected the correct entry and pressed the button to connect me to the dress designer.

It rang three times, the sound filling the car's cozy interior, and was answered.

"Rudyard here, thanks for returning my call, Felicity. So sorry I couldn't get to you today."

I hadn't listened to the message yet – I figured I didn't need to since I knew it was about not being able to get to our two o'clock meeting as planned. It worked in my favour as I wanted to employ my afternoon otherwise.

Thinking I ought to warm up to the subject of me needing him to make a dress super-fast, I said, "That's perfectly okay, Rudyard. We can rearrange to meet in the near future." He clearly thought I had listened to the message and correcting him seemed unnecessary. What I needed to tell him was that Annabelle was dead and his dress had been ruined. Even if the dress had survived intact, I wouldn't dream of letting a bride get married in it. It was last worn by a dead woman!

"We might need to meet sooner than you think," he replied with a cryptic edge to his voice.

Thinking he had no idea how right he was, I said, "Oh? Why is that?"

"Well," I knew Rudyard of old, and have never heard quite so much barely contained excitement in his voice. "When I tried to call you earlier – I was at Kings Cross Station on my way to you ... those darned announcers are so loud. Anyway, I was calling because I wanted you to be the first to know ... wait a moment, are you alone? I don't want anyone else to overhear us?"

My eyes widened a little. What was he about to share with me?

"I'm in my car and my assistant is with me," I explained. "She can be trusted to keep a secret"

Rudyard's attitude shifted. His tone too when he commanded, "State your name, please."

Mindy glanced at me with a questioning look. "Um, Mindy? Mindy Walters."

"Very good, Mindy Walters," Rudyard was speaking directly to her. "This is serious stuff. I need you to swear on your life that you will not breath a word of this to anyone."

Mindy's eyes flared and she silently mouthed a question, asking what it was that she was signing up for.

I spoke up, "I can call you back later if ..."

"No, it's fine," Mindy cut over me. "I swear on my life I will keep this secret until my dying day." Mindy went over the top, miming stabbing herself in the heart as she said the words, but her sarcasm didn't make it across the airwaves.

"Very good. Now, ladies, if you are both listening." We replied that we were. "I can reveal that I heard it from a good source, who has a brother whose girlfriend's mother works at the palace, that the future wife of Prince Marcus," now I got the secrecy because the engagement was yet to be officially announced, "likes my wedding dresses." Rudyard fell silent, leaving space for Mindy and me to make comment.

Mindy was looking at me, unsure why this was such a big secret. It wasn't like he had just taken the order for a dress and would be the designer to clad the next princess in full view of about half the planet.

"Well, what do you think?" he prompted.

Jolted into responding, I gushed, "Oh, that's marvellous, Rudyard!"

"Yeah, wicked!" offered Mindy, changing her voice to sound like a street-cool gangsta.

Shooting her a warning frown, I said, "It's hardly any surprise though, Rudyard. Your dresses are the best out there."

"Oh, stop it," he pretended to be bashful, while making it clear he would listen to me butter his buns all day. Changing back to a serious tone, he said, "Look, I called you first, Felicity, because I know you are being seriously considered for the job of wedding planner."

My heart thumped in my chest. "I am?"

"Oh, don't be coy, Felicity. From what I hear, this is a two-horse race."

Squinting as if to ward off a blow, I asked in an innocent tone, "Who is the other horse?"

Rudyard chuckled. "Your old enemy, Primrose Green. I'm surprised the two of you don't get along better. You have more in common than most people."

I probably would get along with her if she wasn't a conniving cow bent on getting ahead by dragging me down, sullying my name, and generally wishing me ruin.

I was getting lost in a conversation about the royal wedding, and could happily talk for hours about it and what I could do to improve my chances. However, the thing I needed to do right now was prevent the murder of Annabelle Richards being associated with my name.

Steering the conversation away from a topic I wanted to explore, I said, "Rudyard if I am awarded the opportunity to work with the palace to create the royal wedding, you will be the first person I contact. Norma Morley will look stunning in one of your dresses and the world will truly see her as a princess."

"Kind words indeed," he acknowledged. "I hope we work together to make that happen."

Now that he was suitably on my side, I shifted topic.

"I'm glad you called, actually. I'm afraid I have some terrible news for you." I paused, not for dramatic effect, but to give him a few seconds to prepare himself. "Annabelle Richards is dead."

I heard stunned silence for several seconds.

"Annabelle?" he questioned. "But I was just speaking to her yesterday. She sounded healthy and well? Was it an accident?"

I huffed out a frustrated breath, wishing I wasn't the one to be breaking the news. It served a purpose though, leading him to what I hoped he might now do for my brides.

In a quiet, respectful voice, I told him the truth, "Rudyard, I'm afraid to say that she was murdered."

He gasped loudly and there was a distinct clunk before the line went dead.

Mindy skewed her lips to one side, staring at the car's centre console as if it might be to blame.

"That was weird," she remarked.

The phone rang a second later, the screen on the console displaying Rudyard's name. When I thumbed the button to connect him, he was talking instantly.

"Goodness, I'm so sorry. I sort of came over a little faint then and I dropped my phone. Do they know who did it?"

I didn't want to tell him about the brides fighting over his dress.

"The police are investigating." It was a nice, honest, and completely neutral response. "There is another thing I have to tell you."

"Oh?"

"When she was killed, your dress was ruined, I'm afraid." Leaving out the part about Annabelle being posed in the dress felt prudent.

"They ruined my dress?" Rudyard sounded like he just couldn't believe it.

"Yes, the one with the sweetheart A-line ..."

"I know which one it was," he murmured wistfully. "I was never truly happy with it, truth be told. Well, actually I was completely happy with it until that pig Australian imposter, Marc Anthony, released an exact copy a week before mine was due to be unveiled. And he got to do it in the *Catwalk Magazine* wedding edition."

The venom in Rudyard's voice was as sudden as it was startling. "I knew I couldn't publicise it the way I wanted – a whole campaign ruined. If I had, Marc's people would have accused me of copying him. They can be so underhanded."

So that was why the dress was suddenly being given away at a bargain price. Well, bargain price for a Kipling Original. His campaign had been ruined, but his marketing people came up with a new idea to draw attention to his label.

I made suitable sounds of sympathy and agreement though I wasn't going to agree in words because Marc Anthony made amazing dresses and I would be contacting him too if I got the royal wedding job. The bride deserved to have choices.

Getting in quick before he could speak again, I said, "Here's the thing, Rudyard, the dress has been sold and the bride is due to marry in just a couple of weeks. Is there any way you can make a replacement? It doesn't matter if it's not exactly the same …"

"Of course, Felicity," he interrupted me to say the one thing I hadn't expected. "I'll have someone drop it down to you this afternoon."

"Wait. I thought each dress is a one-off?"

Rudyard Kipling had a strict policy of only making each dress once. It was a quirk many thought odd until he sold one to a Hollywood A-lister and demand went through the roof. The price he could command because a bride could buy her special gown secure in the knowledge there would never be another the same was shocking.

Mindy and I heard a snort of amusement. "Well, yes, Felicity. I only sell one dress, but I make spares for magazine shoots and such. The dress gets worn by models and it gets handled. The bride, whoever she may be, wants a dress that hasn't been touched by anyone."

That made total sense. How come, after all my years in the industry, I didn't know designers did that?

I was a little gobsmacked. He was going to drop a dress to me before the end of the day. Problem solved. Or not, I realised because I still only had one dress and at least two brides who had paid a deposit for it. I was yet to get a response from Mary, but it hadn't been all that long since I left her a message.

We were passing West Malling and would arrive at Gertrude's country house in Tudely in a few minutes. If Mary hadn't returned my call by the time we finished, I would detour via her house on the way home.

Quite how I decided which bride got the real Kipling dress and which one had to make do with whatever alternative I came up with, was a problem for later. The alternative would be an amazing dress, but ultimately, it wouldn't be a Kipling Original that came with a magazine shoot.

I expressed my deepest thanks to Rudyard, once again promising to keep him informed regarding my bid to be the royal wedding planner.

With the call ended, I put on my indicator and cruised into the right lane to turn across the road and into the lane that would take me to the village of Tudely. I had to wait for an approaching car to pass, but noticed its indicator come on too. They were taking the same turning.

As the car slowed, and I waited, my eyes caught sight of the driver.

It was Gertrude.

Mindy made a confused face. "I thought you said she was at a spa in West Malling?"

It was precisely what Gertrude had told me. So why was she coming from the opposite direction?

IS GErTruDE GUILTY?

Gertrude swung her steering wheel, steering her vintage Bentley through a wide arc to then power it down the lane into the village beyond. She hadn't seen me; of that I was certain.

I gave it a few seconds, not wanting to follow too closely behind and believing there was no need to keep her in sight because she was on her way home.

A honk from the car behind – I hadn't noticed it because I was watching Gertrude's car – made me jump. I checked my mirrors and the road, waved an apology through my back window, and made my way into Tudely.

Like many of England's villages, Tudely had stood for centuries with few changes other than the appearance of satellite dishes and the expansion of the village boundaries as new houses were added. In the centre one found a traditional village green. Too small for cricket, it was formed by a confluence of ancient tracks that had become roads a century ago with the advent of cars. Bordered by houses around the perimeter, two public houses sat on adjacent corners, their rivalry undoubtedly friendly at times and less so at others.

We passed through the centre, leaving the green, the pubs, and the bulk of houses behind us, emerging from the village to then take a narrow track on the left. This was my third visit to Gertrude Blithe-Leatham's house or, more accurately, her parents' house, and I knew how to get there without needing to think or engage the satnav.

My car's exhaust note changed as the trees formed a tight canopy above us, funnelling the noise back inward as we passed through a dark spot with little natural sunlight. On the other side, the land opened out once more, angling down slightly toward the 16th century farmhouse and stables positioned next to a natural lake.

It was a splendid property Gertrude took great joy in boasting had been in her family for more than two hundred years. As the only daughter she was set to inherit the entire estate and that was probably how she has attracted her groom.

Catching myself thinking negatively about one of my brides, I stopped myself. Yes, she was annoying and bossy. Yes, she was punching above her weight with her fiancé. However, none of that should impact my opinion. I was engaged to provide a high-end service and that very definitely meant zero negativity on my part.

"There's her car." Mindy pointed through the windscreen.

The tail end of her Bentley could be seen inside a carport next to the house. Of Gertrude there was no sign, but we were far enough behind that she would have parked and gone into the house by now.

I parked in an obvious spot next to the car port and lost sight of Mindy before I could get out of the car. I didn't need to see her to know what she was up to; I could hear Buster's thoughts.

"Good idea, Mindy. Let's check the car and then mark the tyres."

"Mindy!" I hissed, keeping my voice to an urgent whisper. My niece could be such an incorrigible snoop and Buster was going to make it obvious we had been doing just that. Okay, it's what we came here for, but peeing on her car did not feel like a necessary step.

"Auntie," Mindy hissed back at me, poking her head around the side of the carport to get my attention. She gestured urgently for me to come to her and vanished inside again.

Feeling like I was trespassing and about to be caught, I glanced all around before sneaking into the open sided building.

The car was a beauty. I'm not what you could call a car person, which is to say that I like what I see, or I don't, but unless it says what it is on it, I haven't got much of a clue what I am looking at.

The word 'Bentley' emblazoned the rear boot lid of the elegant two-seater. If forced to guess, I would say it was from the post war period, sometime in the fifties perhaps. The swooping lines and two-tone paint made the car look like it was in motion even when stationary and it had to cost more than some people's houses.

I couldn't say anything bad about that – the rich were precisely the customers my business was set up to cater for.

Mindy hissed, "Her handbag is on the passenger seat." She was trying the handle, gripping it with a clear intention to open it.

"No, Mindy!" I raced to stop her.

Her hand fell away before I got to her. "It's locked anyway," she muttered, cupping her hands around her face to see inside. "I bet I can force the window down – it's fitted with those strange old winding handles."

That my niece had never used anything other than an electric window spoke volumes about the age gap between us.

Stopping her before she could root through her own handbag to find a tool to jimmy the car's locks, I grabbed her arm and pulled her away.

"We are here to speak with Gertrude, not rob her."

Trailing in my wake, Mindy muttered, "I wasn't going to rob her, just dig through her things to find her dirty secrets."

At the edge of the carport, I poked my head out and looked around. Coast clear, I stepped out, pretending like we hadn't been snooping and went to the front door.

Buster sniffed the air. "*Someone's making soup.*" He sniffed again. "*Carrot and tomato. Do you think …*"

"You don't need any soup, Buster," I hushed him as a shadow fell across the frosted glass of the door.

Gertrude opened it.

"Ah, Mrs Philips. Good. What do you propose to do about my dress?"

It is my opinion that anyone else would have greeted me and offered their hand to shake. In many instances, an air kiss to the cheek would be appropriate. Gertrude was all but tapping her foot as she waited for me to answer.

Mindy, standing just behind my left shoulder, leaned forward to whisper, "I thought you said the brides were getting skinny to fit into the dress?"

I acted as if I hadn't heard a thing. Gertrude had a woman's figure, nothing more or less than that. The fact that the dress in question was a size zero – a size few women on the planet could reach no matter what diet they chose to follow – was another matter entirely. However, though Gertrude was most likely a healthy size ten, and was currently clad in sports clothes to support her claim of coming from the gym, she did look to have put on a few pounds since I last saw her.

Ignoring all that, I answered her question, "I spoke with the designer not half an hour ago, Gertrude. A replacement for the dress will be delivered to my office before the end of the day." Not that Gertrude would fit in it.

Let me be quite clear that I care not one jot for a bride's size or shape. As I may have mentioned earlier, the industry is guilty of perpetually promoting size zero brides and pushing those intending to get married into doing all they can to look just like the pictures in the magazines. It is not as bad as it used to be and there are many stores who now cater openly to the larger lady who, let's be real here, form the bulk of the customer base.

Nevertheless, there was no way Gertrude was ever getting into the Kipling dress.

"Can we talk about this inside, Gertrude?" I asked, a polite smile adding emphasis to how rude she was being.

From somewhere inside the house a woman's voice called, "Who is it, Gertie?"

Gertrude muttered something under her breath before shouting over her shoulder.

"Just the wedding planner, Mum."

"Well let her in, Gertie. I want to meet her."

I thought it said a lot about who Gertrude was as a person that I was yet to meet anyone from her family. I hadn't even met her fiancé, Eddie Thring. Only through the photographs she carried did I have any idea what he looked like.

With obvious reluctance, Gertrude Blithe-Leatham stepped back to grant us entry.

The house was not so much large as it was grand. The rooms were big, and filled with elegant clutter, which is to say there was something in every direction one looked, but it all fitted with the theme of the house. An elephant's foot umbrella stand – a 19th century anachronism stood just inside the door, the sole umbrella in it fitted with a carved wooden duck's head for a handle.

I pulled Buster in tight next to me. He was nothing if not clumsy.

"*That soup sure smells good,*" he remarked.

He was right that there was a scent in the house. My nose was not powerful enough or sufficiently attuned to determine the precise nature of the ingredients. It did smell like vegetables though.

"Maybe I should just try some since we are here. Isn't that what guests do?"

I gave Buster's lead a tug to make him look up at me. I was going to shush him again, but now that he wasn't looking where he was going, he almost walked into a large vase.

I steered him away from it, putting a finger to my lips when he glanced up again.

Gertrude led us past oil paintings that might have been worthless or valued in millions. There were knick knacks and bric-a-brac on every surface: a china bulldog, a pair of original Corgi cars still in their original boxes. It was the home of a collector for sure.

"Admiring the clutterments?" asked Gertrude, tracking my eyes. "The whole lot is going in the trash the moment the old bag pops her clogs. The house will feel twice the size in an instant."

I kept my mouth shut.

Coming into a large sitting room, a lady in her fifties was carefully placing a trio of jade elephants back into a cubby by the fireplace. A feather duster was tucked under her left arm. The first thing I noticed was how unlike her daughter she looked. If there was any family resemblance, I could not see it.

Mrs Blithe-Leatham was half a foot shorter, had darker hair, and was petite. Gertrude got all her features from her father then.

"Did I hear you say something, Gertie?" Her mother's tone suggested she heard exactly what was said and did not approve.

"Just talking about your awful ornaments, Mum."

"Will you just shut up about them, Gertie. This is my house, not yours." Mrs Blithe-Leatham forced her expression, which had been hard when speaking to her daughter, to soften as she turned her eyes toward her guests. She came toward us, holding out both hands to clasp one of mine. You must be Felicity Philips. I've read so much about you. I'm Carol."

"Hello, yes, I'm Felicity. This is my niece, Mindy. She works with me. I'm sure you are aware of the setback with your daughter's dress." I had been curious to know if the police had been to the house, but didn't feel there was a need to ask the question. Had they done so, Carol would surely have raised the point already.

Carol looked from me to Gertrude and back again. "What dress? You said you were yet to pick a dress and that was why we haven't been dress shopping together yet. What is it that I don't know?"

Under her breath, but loud enough for all to hear, Mindy sang, "Awkward."

"Have you picked a dress, Gertrude?" Carol was instantly balling her hands onto her hips.

"It's *my* wedding, Mother. I get to choose what kind of dress I want to wear. I don't need to hear anyone's opinion on the subject."

The women were facing off against each other, squaring up like two boxers about to start exchanging blows.

I backed away a pace, nudging Mindy to get her moving. "We should leave," I whispered.

Mindy wasn't going anywhere, ducking her head to the side to get a clear view of mother and daughter.

"No, Auntie, this is good stuff. I want to see who throws the first punch."

Carol went with the age old, "Who do you think is paying for this wedding, Gertrude?"

Her daughter spat back, "I've got my own money, Mother! I don't need you to pay for it!"

I gave Mindy a shove, the nimble teenager conceding though we both knew she could resist me easily enough.

Carol yelled, "Don't leave!" before I could get halfway across the room. "Someone needs to tell me something about this wedding. Lord knows Gertrude hasn't. I haven't even seen the guest list."

"That's because they are my guests!" Gertrude raged. "You'll just invite stupid relatives and dig out a bunch of cousins I've never even heard of."

I really wanted to get to the part where I carefully quizzed Gertrude about where she was around the time Annabelle was killed, but I also believed we were intruding and ought to give the two ladies some time to figure out their differences.

Trapped by indecision, I said, "Perhaps we ought to come back in a bit?"

The fight went out of Carol, her shoulders drooping as she waved a dismissive hand at her daughter.

"Look, Gertie, I just want to be a part of it, that's all." Her voice was sad and almost begging Gertrude with its tone.

Gertrude was not of a mind to back down even when offered an olive branch. "You want to take over and plan it for me, you mean."

Carol cast her eyes down, either accepting defeat or sensing the futility of continuing to argue.

Turning her eyes to me, Carol asked, "What sort of dress is it?"

Gertrude finally calmed down, the fight going out of her voice now that she appeared to have won. She slowly took her eyes from her mother to look across at Mindy and me.

"Do you have a picture?" the bride enquired.

Caught out momentarily by her request, I floundered for a second. The files I keep for each bride were back at the office.

"Here," said Mindy, offering her phone. "I have a picture of it."

Carol nodded her thanks as she accepted the phone, turning it around to look at the dress.

"It's beautiful," she remarked but we all heard the unspoken 'but' in her words.

Gertrude prompted her, "But."

Carol continued to look at the phone. "This is the actual dress?"

I nodded. "Yes."

She passed the phone back with a murmur of thanks before spearing her daughter with a questioning stare.

"Then how do you propose to get into it, Gertie? That thing can't be any bigger than a size four."

"It's a zero," supplied Mindy unhelpfully.

Carol threw her arms in the air. "Gertie you're a size ten!"

Gertrude wasn't cowed one little bit. "They are going to let the dress out."

I hadn't realised I was waiting for my chance until that exact moment. Without me attempting to steer the conversation, it had come around to us discussing the dress anyway. Gertrude was never going to win the competition and be the first one to fit into it. Had that made her mad enough to kill? She acted as if everyone was beneath her, would the life of a dressmaker matter to her?

"There was a competition, wasn't there?" I interrupted the flow of the Blithe-Leathams' argument. Carol knew nothing of this, so I explained. "The dressmaker's assistant erroneously took three deposits for the same one-off dress. None of the brides would take their deposit back – the dress is rather desirable – so the dressmaker set a competition."

"Competition?" Carol repeated the word. "I don't follow."

Gertrude folded her arms and made a show of looking displeased.

I continued regardless. "Any dress can be stretched to a bigger size – the dressmaker would insert a panel or panels, but the most they could stretch it by is two dress sizes, three at the absolute maximum. Any more than that and the dress would be ruined. Annabelle Richards, the lady who was selling the dress, challenged the three brides to drop down to a size four."

Carol scoffed, "Ha! Well, you were never going to manage that, were you. You haven't even been trying."

"I didn't need to get skinny. I was going to win anyway. I had a special arrangement."

Now I was lost.

"What does that mean?"

Put on the spot, Gertrude finally showed an emotion other than arrogance as her cheeks tinged with pink.

"It means ... it means. Never you mind what it means." The arrogant version of Gertrude wasn't gone for long. "I'm not paying you to interrogate me."

"*Shall I bite her?*" asked Buster.

I wanted to press Gertrude on the dress, but her mother asked another question. An even better one than I could have hoped for.

"Where have you been all day anyway?"

Gertrude's jaw was in motion, her mouth set to deliver a comment about something else when it froze and closed.

I listened intently for her answer, all eyes on her and no one saying a word.

"Well?" Carol prompted.

Gertrude lifted her arms in a big display to draw attention to her outfit.

"I went to the gym. Isn't it obvious? I'm supposed to be getting skinny, remember? Isn't that what we were just talking about?"

Mindy remarked, "That's not how I look when I have been to the gym." She was right. Gertrude's makeup was flawless and her stretchy gym clothes were bone dry – no trace of sweat anywhere.

Gertrude shot her a bored look. "They have shower rooms at the kind of gym I can afford to go to. I got changed and did my hair and makeup before I left."

"Which gym did you go to?" I pressed her, believing she was lying and not wanting to let up the pressure.

Her eyes twitched across to me, her expression disdainful because I was getting too big for my boots.

"Pure Body in West Malling, thank you very much."

I was treading on thin ice. If Gertrude was Annabelle's killer, then I wanted to know – this was about protecting my business. However, if she wasn't the killer, I was damaging my reputation and undoubtedly losing a client and all the recommendations that would normally follow. I nevertheless chose to fire in my next question.

"Then how was it you were coming into the village from Tonbridge direction?"

Again, Gertrude's cheeks tinged pink, as caught in her lie, she couldn't think of anything to say.

"What time did you leave the house this morning, Gertrude?" I pressed.

My latest question triggered something.

"What? How dare you? Who do you think you are to be asking me questions?"

Carol supplied the answer in defiance of her daughter. "It was just after eleven o'clock."

The pink in her cheeks went full crimson as the needle in her rage meter shot all the way to the top.

"Mrs Philips you are fired. I have no further use for a wedding planner who cannot keep her nose out of my business."

Carol sprang to my defence.

"You cannot fire your wedding planner less than a month before the event, Gertie."

"Yes, I can, Mother."

This wasn't what I wanted, but it did release me to go for broke.

"Did you strangle Annabelle Richards? Did you believe you were going to get the dress and see red when Annabelle told you it was going to someone else? Have the police tracked you down yet? I'm sure they will have questions regarding your whereabouts and movements around noon today."

My direct question made Gertrude's eyes bug out, but the bigger reaction came from Carol.

"What! What did you just ask my daughter?"

I kept my eyes on Gertrude, but she was looking at me now with a satisfied smirk. Only then did I sense my error – I had pushed too hard and inadvertently caused the mumma bear instinct to awaken. Carol was the problem now.

"I think my daughter is right, Mrs Philips. It is time you left. Your services will no longer be required."

I said several rude words in my head. This was not what I wanted at all.

Gertrude took a pace forward and Buster growled a warning. I think she only intended to point to the door and send me on my way, but getting too close to my personal space she triggered Buster's defence mechanisms.

Carol snapped, "Get your dog under control!"

Hauling him back, I nodded to Mindy – we were leaving.

Continuing to talk as I made my way back to their front door, Carol said, "You can send a bill for the hours so far, Mrs Philips. I expect, however, for you to remain professional and pass us the details of everything that has been arranged. I will be contacting a different wedding planner to take over. I should imagine that will cost me something extra at such short notice, but that is the position we find ourselves in," she lamented.

Gertrude said, "There was another lady I almost hired. She expressed that she could step in at any point if I felt Mrs Philips wasn't cutting it. She seemed to expect it, in fact."

"You have her name?" Carol quizzed.

I knew what Gertrude was going to say so it came as no shock.

"Primrose Green."

I cracked my knuckles.

"Very good. Why don't you call her now, Gertie? I will see Mrs Philips out."

Mindy was already at the door, turning the handle to let herself out. Buster followed her, leading me back out and onto the front steps. I turned to express to Carol my concern over the death of Annabelle, but got the door shut in my face.

"Well, that was rude." Mindy looked cross. "Do you think she did it, Auntie?"

Heck yes, I did.

The question then was what to do about it. I could call the police and alert them to my suspicions. They would soon find the names of the brides and come to question them – I had only got here first because I had the information in advance. However, keeping my name away from the police and most especially the press, was the entire point of trying to figure this out for myself.

Surreptitiously gesturing for Mindy to come with me, I started walking back toward my car.

"Are we just going to leave, Auntie?" Mindy begged to know. "What if she killed Annabelle?"

I glanced to my right, looking, but not staring, through the windows of the lower floor. Carol and

Gertrude were inside somewhere. Were they watching me? I had to assume they could see me and would notice if I did anything other than go back to my car. Fortunately, the edge of the house would eclipse me before I got there. They would expect to hear my car and see it going down the driveway, but I doubted they would come outside to investigate in the next couple of minutes.

The moment we walked out of sight, I ran to the edge of the house and peered around to see back inside.

Buster could sense I was up to something.

"Is it Devil Dog time? Do I need to bust down the door and drag them both out?"

I shushed him.

"We need to be quiet."

"Yeah, quiet. Got it. Devil Dog and quiet go together like darkness and the moon."

I reached down to clamp a hand over his mouth because he was still making growling sounds.

Mindy was right next to my ear when she spoke.

"What are we doing, Auntie?"

"Trying to spot them. Carol kicked us out, but what do you think she did next? She had no idea where Gertrude was this morning. She's in there now quizzing her, I'd bet the company on it."

A flash of movement deep in the house drew our eyes. It was hard to see anything – looking into a dark building from the daylight outside, but we could tell someone was heading to the kitchen at the rear of the house.

"Come on. I'm going to see if there is a window open." I peeled away from the wall, heading for a side gate between the car port and the house.

Mindy followed. "Goodness, Auntie, you're so badass these days. You weren't like this at all when I started working for you."

Her observation gave me pause. She was right, my attitude towards certain things had changed or rather it had been changed for me by circumstance.

In the last couple of months – ever since I met up with Patricia Fisher after not seeing her for many years, people had been dropping dead. That wasn't accurate though. They were not dropping dead, other people had killed them. The latest was Annabelle. Not that I believed Patricia Fisher was a factor, but a sense of desperation was leading me to take steps I would never have considered before all this started happening.

Questioning whether I ought to just get into my car and leave, I continued to sneak around the side of the house.

At the next corner, we both peered around to see if the coast was clear. Straining my hearing, I could detect what sounded like a thin stream of water hitting a hard surface under pressure. Whatever it was, it was out of sight.

I was about to step out into the garden, planning to creep beneath the window to the kitchen to then peer inside, but didn't want to get my trousers soaked walking in front of a leaking hose or whatever it was.

Mindy grabbed my ribs on either side and jerked me to one side.

"Ewww, Buster!" she complained.

My dog looked up as I looked down. The water under pressure noise wasn't a leaking hose, it was Buster taking a leak.

"What? I needed to go. At least I don't do it in the house like you humans. Your habits are disgusting."

With a nod of thanks to Mindy who had shifted me out of the way of the yellow stream heading for my feet, I took an exaggerated step to get over it and crouched to sidle under the windows.

There *was* a window open. It was ten yards away, the muscles in my legs and back beginning to protest by the time I got there. No such problem for Mindy, the nimble little ninja, or for Buster who was shin height to me and couldn't reach the window ledge even standing on his back feet.

Yet again, to hear what was being said inside required me to strain my hearing, but the two women were good enough to be having a heated discussion, their voices raised accordingly.

"It's none of your business where I was, Mother."

Carol wasn't going to be diverted easily. "I rather think it is. If this Annabelle was murdered this morning, and you have business with her, the police are going to come calling. Isn't that what Mrs Philips claimed?"

"She doesn't know what she is talking about and neither do you. Besides, wherever I was, which is still none of your business, I wasn't in Rochester strangling some second-rate seamstress."

"So where were you, Gertie?" Carol persisted. "You clearly weren't at the gym."

"Yes, I was."

"Oh, please, Gertie. I'm your mother. Don't you think I learned to tell when you are lying a long time ago?"

The doorbell ringing stopped their conversation.

"That will probably be the police right now," remarked Carol. "You'll need to get your story straight for them."

I couldn't tell if her mother's comment might have sent a spike of panic through Gertrude's heart, but it certainly did mine. Was it the police? We were trespassing and eavesdropping, and while these were not crimes I would get arrested for, it would not look good if we were caught. Plus, what if it was Chief Inspector Quinn at the door? What if he caught me snooping?

My legs were starting to shake from holding the crouch. I couldn't kneel without getting my knees wet and dirty. Flapping an arm at Mindy to get her moving, I hissed, "Back to the car."

She took off, walking in a crouch as if it was nothing. Were my knees ever that supple? Were my thighs ever that strong? I knew the answer was yes – years as a ballerina provided both those attributes. The same discipline also hammered the cartilage in my ankles, knees, and hips which was why shuffling along behind the house was so hard now.

"Pppsssssttttlghh"" Buster sneezed. It was the type of sneeze only a creature with a snubby little nose like a bulldog can pull off and when viewed was much akin to seeing the insides of his head attempt to escape through his nostrils.

Now filled with the fear of getting caught, I had to will my legs to move faster. I was still crouching, unable to stand for that would instantly expose me, but I could hear footsteps moving fast across the kitchen tile.

The back door proved to be my salvation. Gertrude had to fight the lock and finally got the door open just as I slipped around the edge of the house and out of sight.

Mindy wasn't there waiting for me. She was at the other end, peeking around the corner.

"They just went inside," she told me. "Did Gertrude spot you?"

I checked over my shoulder. If anyone was following, they would have been on us by now.

I shook my head. "I guess not."

"Perfect. Let's check her car then."

With confident strides, Mindy stepped out from the lee of the building, walking on her toes to stop her heels clicking on the path as she went directly to the car port again.

"We know the Blithe-Leathams are inside now," she explained. "The police will keep them busy, so we have at least a couple of minutes to check her handbag and phone."

"What if she decides she needs her phone and comes out to get it?" I challenged.

Mindy needed only a second of thought. "You can tell Buster to hide under her car. If anyone leaves the house, I'll quickly put everything back as it was and get on the ground to pretend I'm trying to coax him out."

Buster would have saluted if he could. "*Devil Dog ready for duty.*"

I didn't have a worthwhile argument to raise and all the crazy risk taking so far had been my idea. While

I kept watch and let Buster off his lead, Mindy edged down the side of the car, looking for a way to open it.

"I think all I need to do is get my fingers under the fabric of the hood. Oh, wait a minute, the handbag's gone," she reported in surprise. "And the door is unlocked now."

I took a step forward to see for myself, taking my eyes off the world outside which is why I didn't see the shadow detach itself from the log pile in the corner and come toward me.

UNWELCOME AMBUSH

"**W**WA-HA-HA-HAAAAA!"

I shot into the air, my heart stopping instantly as in a fight or flight reflex, I jumped backward to get away from my attacker. Mindy was two feet behind me, and unmoveable it seemed because I hit her and bounced right off. Stumbling forward and thus back toward the person who had hidden in ambush, I got to hear Mindy burst into hysterical laughter right before Vince caught me.

I was off balance and going to fall, but landing on my knees, rump, or face would have been preferable to being touched, thank you very much.

I fought him off even as he tried to stand me upright.

"I got you a good un," he sniggered, reaching down to ruffle Buster's fur as he fussed around Vince's feet.

Mindy was cackling with him. "You sure did. How's your heart, Auntie?"

I wanted to say that it had elected to stop working and was going to remain on strike until I started getting a little more respect. Mercifully, I could still feel it beating, if somewhat erratically, in my chest.

Vince was still within thumping distance, so that was exactly what I did, whacking him on the meaty part of his right arm with all the force I could muster. I might as well have not bothered for all the difference it made.

"Passion. That's what I like most about you, Felicity. You've got such fire in you."

I was giving serious consideration to kicking him in the trousers.

"I take it you were looking for this?" he held Gertrude's handbag aloft.

Mindy looked down at the car door. "How did you get the car open?"

With a slick motion, Vince extended his right arm. A thin, flat metal rod slid out from his jacket sleeve.

"Tools of the trade, Mindy."

"That's a thief's tool," I accused him.

He chuckled. "Only if one employs it to steal things."

"What do you call the handbag hanging from your left hand?" I felt I was making a pertinent point.

He cast his eyes in its direction "This? This isn't stolen, darling. I performed an illegal search to obtain it, but once I put it back, no 'actual' crime has been committed. Anyway, there's nothing of interest in her handbag and I cloned the phone's memory chip so we can check all her calls, contacts, and movements at our leisure."

Mindy was in awe. "You can do that?"

Vince was modest in his reply. "Sure. All P.I.s can."

Buster nudged my leg. "*Devil Dog needs one of those. It can go on my utility collar.*"

"That's so cool." Mindy was equally impressed.

Buster nudged my leg again. "*Do you need to write that down? Or will you just remember? The utility collar will probably need a battery pack and some charging ports to keep all my gadgets ready to go.*"

Vince said, "We should probably not hang around for too long. I would have put this back already if you hadn't shown up." He threw the handbag to Mindy, who caught it, dropped it into the car, and pushed the door closed.

"We should lock it again, right?" she asked.

I looked at her for a second, questioning why she didn't just do it herself and then realised she had never been in a car without central locking. I could have explained it, but that would take longer than doing it myself.

"*Utility collar*," Buster spoke a little louder. "*With charging ports*."

Accepting that Buster wasn't going to let this go, I looked down at him.

"Okay, Buster. We'll talk about it later."

He wiggled his tail. "*Cool. I wonder what else I can get to go on it*."

Now that I was able to move on, I indicated that I needed to get to the car. Mindy had to step out of my way, and then watched in wonder as I opened Gertrude's car door, pushed down the button inside, and closed the door again while holding up the handle on the outside.

"That was like magic," she gasped.

I wasn't hanging around to explain it - it was long past our time to be elsewhere, and I still hoped to catch Mary at home.

Heading for my car, Buster trotting gamely in front, I spotted the big incongruity.

"Where's your car?" That my question was aimed at Vince did not need to be explained.

He pointed across a field. "Hidden. First rule of being a P.I. – stay invisible. I could do with a lift back to it though."

I shot him a happy smile. "Sorry. Two-seater." I indicated my little Mercedes.

"We could squeeze in," he suggested with a leer. "I'll sit on the passenger seat, and you can sit on my lap."

"I don't mind driving," volunteered Mindy who was always angling to get a shot at driving my sports car.

I made shooing motions across the field.

"I would say that I am tempted, Mr Slater, at your offer to let me sit on your lap, but I'm not. Not even slightly." Opening my car door, I paused with one foot inside. "Be sure to let me know what you find on Gertrude's phone, won't you." I knew he would, and that he would call me asking to deliver whatever he found in person. That wasn't going to happen. Vince Slater had gotten close enough to me already. He was sweet – sort of – but best kept at arm's length.

He was still watching to see if I would change my mind when I angled my car around and powered up the driveway. Ahead of us the sun was racing toward the horizon and the shadows cast by the trees were getting long.

When I expressed my plan to swing via Mary's house on our way back to the office, Mindy saw fit to question it.

"Surely Gertrude is the killer, Auntie? We know she lied about going to the gym. She was out of the house early enough this morning to get to Rochester in time to kill Annabelle. And we know she was never going to get into that dress."

"She also said something about having already won the competition," I reminded myself as well as my niece. "She made some kind of special arrangement. Wasn't that what she said?"

"Which she then refused to explain," Mindy highlighted a key fact. She was silent for a moment, breathing through her nose as she bit her top lip and racked her brains. Out of the blue, she announced,

"I'm going to call Clara again. Maybe she knows something, and I want to check how she is doing anyway. Would we have a place for her at the business, Auntie? I guess she is out of a job."

I had already considered the young woman's employment status but having already taken on Philippe without having anything for him to actually do, the last thing I needed was another mouth to feed.

Thankfully, Mindy had already pressed the dial button on her phone, so I was saved from answering her question by Clara picking up. I got to listen to Mindy's half of the conversation.

"Hi, Clara. How are you doing?"

There was a pause while Mindy listened to whatever Clara was saying.

"Yes, of course. It's terrible." Mindy's voice was filled with sympathy. Seeing that I was trying to hear, Mindy took the phone away from her ear and thumbed the speaker button.

".... going to do now," wailed Clara. "I haven't got any qualifications. Annabelle was teaching me, but I ... I don't want to start working in a supermarket or a fast-food chain. That sounds awful." She struggled to get the words out and what she did say was hard to understand.

"You mustn't worry, babes," Mindy tried to reassure her. "Something will come up. I'm sure Mrs Philips will have a few names she can give you. There are lots of dressmakers around."

This was significantly better than trying to employ her myself and Mindy was right; I did have lots of contacts. Any one of them might be looking for a partly-trained apprentice.

"Really?" Clara sounded like it was too much to hope for.

Mindy glanced at me, and I chose to respond myself.

"Absolutely, Clara. So don't worry too much right now. I do have a question for you though as we try to sort out the mess left behind by the Kipling wedding dress."

"Right. Golly. How Can I help?" Clara sounded instantly brighter.

Mindy licked her lips, figuring out how to word things. "Well, my auntie was able to secure a replacement dress, but we still have to figure out which bride to give it to. We met with Gertrude

Blithe-Leatham this afternoon and she mentioned that she had made a special arrangement and the dress was going to be hers no matter how much weight the other girls lost. Do you know what she might have meant by that?"

"No. Goodness, no. No idea at all."

I exchanged a glance with Mindy. Clara had been far too fast to reply and far too strenuous in putting her point across. She was lying; I would bet money on it.

Mindy pressed her, but didn't call her out. "Is it something Annabelle might have arranged?"

Again Clara was fast to respond. "I really couldn't say. It might have been, I suppose. Look, sorry, I really must go. Thanks for thinking of me. I hope I can come by the shop and get some of those names in the next day or so, that would be really helpful. Bye."

Just like that the line went dead. Clara's whole attitude shifted the moment we asked her about Gertrude's special arrangement.

Mindy let her hands fall into her lap with the screen of her phone facing upward.

"That was weird."

I agreed, and said, "She's hiding something."

Mindy frowned, still staring at her phone. "What could she possibly have to hide? Did she kill Annabelle? Was she doing something she shouldn't have been, and Annabelle found out?"

"Taking back handers," I jumped to what I thought was a logical conclusion.

Mindy gasped. "That makes total sense. She contacts Gertrude or speaks to her in the shop or something. Gertrude wants the dress and money is nothing to her." She made that painfully obvious earlier. "So Clara, on a paltry wage as a dressmaker's assistant makes a little on the side to make sure the dress goes to Miss Blithe-Leatham."

"But how was she going to make sure that happened?" I pointed out the major flaw in her plan. "The dress wasn't hers. Unless Annabelle was in on it, which she wouldn't have been if Clara was taking a backhander, Gertrude's hope of getting the dress never changed."

"That would have made her mad if she found out." Mindy highlighted.

There was motive and opportunity. People were lying and money had very possibly been changing hands. Clara was in the thick of it, of that I felt certain, but we were going to have to get to her later because I was just about to pull up outside the home of Mary Challis.

MARY AND HER MOTHER

Mary Challis was just getting home when we pulled up. Of the three brides, she was the one with a job. I suspected the grand nature of the wedding being planned, and my fees for pulling it all together, were a stretch. However, I also knew Mary was not the one paying the bills.

Mary worked in graphical design, one of a team of five who all co-owned the business. They were friends from university who all chose to go in together. She was marrying one of the other partners, a nice chap called Clarke. There was a sixth partner – the one who put up the money to get the business off the ground – Mary's mother, Hilda.

Hilda spoke for Mary every single time I ever asked the bride a question and glared at Clarke every time he stepped in to make her let Mary speak for herself. It was not my business to know, and I didn't ask, but seeing Mary and her mother arrive home together in the same car now, I had to guess that Mary put up with Hilda brow-beating her at work too.

Due to be married in just under three weeks, on a Tuesday because that was when they could book the venue they wanted and because it cost significantly less on a weekday, the ceremony itself was a quiet event at their local parish church. It was the reception for four hundred guests afterward where all the money was being spent. I knew the driving force behind the lavish nature of the party was Mary's mother, and if anyone in Mary's party could be guilty of murder, Hilda would be the first on my list.

Mary saw Mindy, Buster, and me getting out of my car, her face wrinkling in confusion.

"Come along, Mary!" snapped her mother. "Stop daydreaming, girl. You're always dawdling. No wonder you get so little done at work."

Flustered and embarrassed, Mary gathered a pile of things from the backseat, loading herself down with laptops, files, and a bag of shopping which she looped through one arm and carried on her elbow.

Hilda's hands were empty save for a handbag.

"What are you looking at, Mary? Stop dawdling. I want to get inside."

I was crossing the street, Buster leading the way as usual.

Suddenly becoming aware that there was someone else in the street, Hilda twisted her neck to look our way and tutted.

"I do hope you have resolved the issue with Mary's dress, Mrs Philips," she made it sound like a command.

"What issue?" asked Mary, still loaded down, and looking like she was struggling.

Dismissively, Hilda replied, "It's nothing you need to concern yourself with, Mary."

Frowning now, Mary tried to stand up for herself. "It's *my* dress, Mum."

Hilda's response was instant. "That I am paying for."

"Only because you insisted I had to have the stupidly expensive one," muttered Mary.

It was a cue for Hilda to turn on her. "What would you have gone for? Hmmm? Something off the peg?

That sounds about right. You insist on marrying a man without money, you could at least try to not embarrass me by turning up to the reception wearing a rag."

Vile remark delivered, and her daughter suitably silenced, Hilda swung her attention back to me as I arrived where they stood.

"So?" she demanded. "Have you been able to resolve the matter?"

I wasn't quite sure what was going on. I called Mary's phone and left her the message about the dress, but she didn't seem to know anything about it. Hilda, who would have been in the dark unless her daughter included her in the information, appeared to be fully informed.

To provide an answer and move forward, I said, "Yes. The designer is dropping a replacement dress off today."

"It is another Kipling?" Hilda snapped out her question.

"Yes."

"An exact replica?"

"Yes."

"Good. I shall expect a discount after all this messing about."

Mary managed to get a word in quickly. "Can we get inside, Mum. This is heavy?"

Hilda rolled her eyes. "Oh, do stop whining, Mary."

As we trudged down their garden path – they lived in a pleasant, detached bungalow with mature garden on all sides, I did my best to explain.

"The dressmaker was murdered this morning, Mrs Challis."

Mary stopped dead.

"Oh, my goodness! What happened?"

Tutting at the delay, Hilda took the keys from her daughter and opened the door. Inside, Mary was finally able to offload her arms. Mindy helped, the two women separating the pile which went onto a side table in the hall. Mary carried the bag into the kitchen, following her mother.

Buster snuffled along behind her, always happy to investigate anywhere that might contain food.

"*I can smell evil,*" he warned.

Unsure what that meant, I paused in their hallway, checked to see if anyone was watching, and crouched so we could whisper.

"Evil?" In my head I imagined he could somehow smell Hilda's guilt like there are dogs who can detect when a person has cancer just by smelling them. That wasn't what this was.

Buster narrowed his eyes. *"Yes, evil. Otherwise known as a cat."*

Rolling my eyes, I came out of my crouch.

In the kitchen, Mary was unpacking.

"Can you tell me what happened to Mrs Richards, please?" she begged.

I explained about how I discovered Annabelle while avoiding any unnecessary detail and questioned whether the police had been in contact yet.

The question drew a frown and a sigh. Meek and mild she might be. Under her mother's thumb too, but Mary's ire was rising.

Raising her voice so it would be heard elsewhere in the house she shouted, "Mother? Mother I need my phone."

Mindy took a turn in frowning, disbelief colouring her words when she asked, "Your mother has your phone?"

Mary's cheeks reddened. "She says it is a distraction in the workplace. I can have it in the evenings. Mum believes I should have no need to communicate with anyone when I am at work because she is there and so is Clarke."

Mindy wasn't ready to let that go. "And you allow her to do that?"

The question clicked Mary's ire up one more notch and there was a little fire in her voice when she shouted again.

"Mother!"

Hilda walked into the room a moment later.

"What is our rule about shouting in the house? Your father will be home soon. I do hope you will have gotten a grip of yourself by then."

"Where is my phone, Mother? People have been trying to get hold of me all day."

"No one important has called, Mary. There was a voicemail from Mrs Philips which, had I relayed to you, would have distracted you for the rest of the day. There were some other calls, but from unknown numbers and we don't answer those, do we, Mary?" Mary glared at her mother. "No, we do not." Hilda answered her own rhetorical question. "So let's not pretend you are suddenly popular or interesting, Mary, it's so tiresome."

Distinctly irked and happy to show it, Mary walked to the refrigerator from which she extracted a bottle of white wine.

Hilda returned the glare with interest. "I do hope you are not thinking of drinking that, Mary Alice Challis."

"So what if I am, mother?" It was the second time in a few hours Mindy and I had found ourselves in the midst of a mother/daughter dispute. "I'm a grown woman. I can have a glass of wine if I want one."

Hilda was already moving, crossing the kitchen to get to her daughter but with the unhurried pace of a tired parent. Mary lifted the bottle to her lips, dispensing with the need for a glass, but just as she tipped the bottle back, Hilda snatched it from her grasp.

The barest sip that Mary managed to get, shot from her mouth in shock, dribbling down her chin and onto her top.

Hilda sighed, "What an embarrassment you are. This is why I have to control your life, Mary. That boyfriend ..."

"Fiancé!"

"... won't hang around for long if you act like this for him, Mary. I can assure you of that."

"Give me that bottle," Mary growled out the words with barely contained rage.

"You are losing weight, remember? I'm not the one who ate too much and couldn't fit in the wedding dress, am I?"

Beaten back down with what had to be an old argument, Mary lowered her head. "I could have picked a different dress."

"Yes, you probably would have. You're plain enough as it is, Mary. The dress will draw some attention away from your face if nothing else."

Needled and insulted in front of guests, I couldn't tell if Mary was going to cry and run from the room or pick up a meat tenderiser and kill her mother.

Under any other circumstances, I would have left seconds after their conversation began. However, in the interest of trying to figure out who could be behind Annabelle's murder, this was solid gold.

With her head still down, Mary murmured almost inaudibly, "The dress doesn't fit me, mother."

A snort of amusement left Hilda's nose. "Hence the no wine policy, you silly girl. Just a few more pounds and you will have shifted enough of your excess fat for the dress to be let out without it being ruined."

"The dressmaker was murdered," Mary lifted her face again. "Have you no respect for anyone, mum? The poor woman is dead. The competition to fit into the dress is over."

Hilda wasn't put off one little bit.

"And yet it isn't. Is it, Mrs Philips?" She speared me with a look that demanded I confirm her claim.

I wasn't going to do that. "I will soon have a replacement dress, but I will not be holding some awful body-shaming, fat-loss contest to determine who gets it."

Hilda's eyebrows showed her interest. "Oh? And what is it that you propose as a method to determine the recipient? You wish to rinse some more money out of us, I assume." Her tone was haughty and accusatory.

I had met Mary's mother several times before. She always spoke for her daughter. Not so much when Clarke was around, but at all other times. However, I had not until now seen just how vile of a person she was.

"The dress is not mine to sell," I replied calmly. "I believe one of the brides, or a person immediately associated with the brides, is responsible for Annabelle's murder."

My statement shocked Mary, but she didn't look at me. She looked at her mother.

I continued with what I was saying. "The competition created a whirlpool of insanity, sucking those who would covet such an item into taking extraordinary measures to get their hands on it. I will *give* the dress to the bride who most deserves it *and* will fit into it." I looked directly at Mary when I asked, "Do you want the Kipling dress?"

"Yes, she does," snapped Hilda, not wanting to risk Mary answering for herself.

Mary allowed herself a moment to think, but needed only a couple of seconds to decide. She shook her head slowly from side to side.

"No, Felicity. It doesn't suit me. There were other designs I preferred, and it will be cold in that dress at this time of the year. I'm going to pick something with sleeves."

"Sleeves!" shrieked Mary's mother. "Over my dead body."

Mary snatched the bottle of wine back from her mother, glaring at her once more. "If you insist."

Hilda gasped and I had to wonder if this was the first time Mary had truly stood up to her. With their argument at an end, even if it was only a temporary one, I fired in a question.

"Did you travel to work together this morning?"

Both women looked my way.

"Why do you ask," Hilda replied without answering.

"Yes, we did," said Mary once she'd drained a good twenty percent of the bottle. "Did my mother kill Annabelle?"

I had been about to ask another question, one which might carefully lead the ladies into telling me where they worked and what their movements were this morning around the time when Annabelle was killed.

I didn't suspect Mary, though I was prepared to believe she might be carrying so much pent-up rage she could do anything if suitably provoked. Hilda though - she came across as a person who would think nothing of killing Annabelle if it meant she got her own way.

Hilda reacted to her daughter's question with utter outrage.

"How dare you!"

Mary took another swig of wine. "Where did you go for lunch, mum? You usually eat at the office so you can make sure everyone is adhering strictly to the appointed break time. I'm such a lamb I let you boss me around all the time, but I can't for the life of me now figure out why."

"Because if you don't toe the line, you'll be out on your ear," Hilda warned. "At home and at work."

Mary swallowed another mouthful of wine, holding the bottle by the neck and unwilling to put it down in case something happened to it.

Folding her arms with the bottle clutched tightly to her chest, Mary said, "That sounds about right. You're so desperate for control, so used to being a bully and getting your own way, you would kick your own daughter out of her home and fire her from her job." Mary fell silent, looking down and also into the future, I thought. Hilda thought she had won, but Mary wasn't done talking. "Okay. So, for starters, I quit."

"You can't quit. You need the job if you are planning to move in with that useless boyfriend of yours."

Calmly, Mary said, "Clarke is my fiancé, and he is far from useless. He will quit too, I imagine, seconds after I tell him I have. So will Sarah, Harry, and the others. We'll all quit. You can own the company mother, it's your money behind it as you are always telling us, but we will start a new one."

Hilda spat, "You can't! I ... you don't know how."

Mary smiled. "No, but I bet we can figure it out. As for kicking me out, I'm leaving. Just as soon ..." she held up the bottle to inspect the contents, "as I have finished this. Now give me my phone, you cantankerous old cow." Hilda reacted as if slapped. "I need to call Clarke."

This was great, I suppose, from the perspective of a downtrodden woman finally finding her path to freedom. How much of a hand we had played in that I wasn't sure, but we were no closer to finding out where Hilda went this morning.

I decided to try to find out for myself.

"Can you explain your movements between noon and one o'clock this afternoon, Mrs Challis?" It was the wrong thing to ask. Or maybe it wasn't, and it wouldn't have mattered what words came out of my mouth.

The fact that I spoke broke the spell and shifted Hilda's attention. Her daughter was defying her, and there didn't appear to be anything she could do about it. I was a different case entirely.

Her features were contorted with frustrated rage when she looked my way.

"This is your fault, Mrs Philips. Some wedding planner you are. You're fired!"

IF THE DRESS FITS ...

T rudging back to the car, Buster leading eagerly as always, I felt a sense of defeat. So far in my quest to stay ahead of the potential PR nightmare I had lost two clients. My rivals would step in, further weakening my position as the top wedding planner in the country.

Hilda had booted us out of the house, her daughter, Mary, doing nothing to stop her. Admittedly, Mary was well on her way to being three sheets to the wind and had raided her mother's handbag to find her phone. When we left, she was engaged in a raucously loud, and animated conversation with her fiancé. The subject of which was mostly to do with what they were going to do with each other when she got to his place.

I certainly didn't get any kind of answer regarding Hilda's movements around the time of Annabelle's murder, and Mary was too preoccupied with changing her life to care if her mother was a killer.

The police had been attempting to contact Mary, but either hadn't gotten around to trying her place of work, or were yet to uncover enough details about her to know they would find her there. They would appear at her house this evening I felt sure. She might be gone by then, but if someone in the Challis house was a killer, I doubted it was Mary.

Going around to her side of the car, Mindy said, "This has not been the best day ever."

I agreed but didn't bother to vocalise my thoughts. Instead, I said, "We need to head back to the office. At least we don't have to think too hard about who gets the dress now." I only had one bride left.

"What if Donna Moscovitch is the killer?"

Mindy's words were like a slap to the face. If that was the case, I now had no weddings in the next month apart from the one on the cruise ship. Thank goodness for Patricia Fisher.

Slipping into the car after Buster as he bounded across my seat and onto Mindy's lap, I said, "Let us hope that is not the case, Mindy. It will be hard to pay Christmas bonuses if there is no money in the business."

My comment drove home the importance of continual customer churn.

We drove in near silence, neither of us having much to say as we replayed the last few hours. I wondered whether things would be as bleak if I had just stayed in the office and worked. Primrose was bound to get Gertrude's wedding and would go out of her way to let everyone know how badly I failed the bride.

I could hear her annoying voice in my head. "Would you believe that crazy woman Felicity Philips actually turned up at the bride's house and accused her of murder?"

It wouldn't matter that it was factually incorrect. No one would care. It would be seen as juicy gossip and thus ripe to be passed around.

Catching myself in the unnecessary and unjustified act of feeling sorry for myself, I forced the image of Annabelle into my head. Hanging limply from the mannequin stand - she was the victim here, not me.

I wasn't sure what I could do to help figure out which of the three brides was behind it, but the day was coming to an end, and I was feeling weary. I would willingly push through my fatigue if I could think of anything constructive to do about poor Annabelle. As it was, I suspected my best move was to get some sleep and allow my brain some time to consider who had the most to gain by her death.

Also, there was Clara. Annabelle's assistant was guilty of something. The more I thought about it, the more I questioned whether Clara could be Annabelle's killer. She walked into the shop moments after me and was very quick in her bid to convince witnesses that I was behind the murder.

Why did she jump to that conclusion so swiftly? Was it because Clara killed her boss? Had Annabelle found out Clara was taking the customer's money with false promises? I could visualise it in my head. Annabelle threatens to sack Clara. Clara kills Annabelle, and panicking does her best to make it look like a crime of rage or passion by posing the body. Then she goes out and watches for someone to arrive. That someone just happened to be me. She waited a minute, then pounced and screamed blue murder.

Did it fit? Could Clara be behind it? I genuinely had no idea. Experience over the last few weeks had taught me that when it came to figuring out who was behind a crime, I was utterly useless. I always got it wrong.

The lights of Rochester filled my windscreen as I drove around behind the castle and into my parking spot by the office. The lights were still on inside as they should be - Justin and Philippe still working, but about to finish as the end of office hours approached.

What they were most likely working on was the imminent weddings, two of which had just been taken away from me. I needed to break that news at the very least.

I shifted the gear stick into park, set the handbrake and gathered my handbag as I prepared to exit the car. Buster was on his back legs, headbutting the passenger's door in his excitement. Mindy grabbed the door handle to open it, but as she did so a car angled into the parking space right next to her.

I was getting out myself and was surprised to see that it was Rudyard who had just pulled up. He was at the wheel of a new car or one I hadn't seen him in before at least. I thought he drove a Ferrari, but today he was in an Aston Martin convertible; dark metallic grey with a contrasting deep red hood.

He was delivering the dress in person?

I guess he sensed that he was being watched, because he turned to look at us. He gave a sort of smile and rolled his eyes - a universal expression of weariness and the battle to get done everything that must be done.

He grabbed for his door handle at the exact same moment as me. Exiting onto the cobbles, his head appearing above the car roofline, he waved me a greeting.

"Hello, Felicity. I suppose you are wondering what I am doing here in person. I decided that since we needed to rearrange our meeting, and the royal wedding is at the top of my priority list ... plus, of course someone had to deliver the dress."

I would never have asked, but it was true that I was expecting an assistant and not the designer. It was supposed to be nothing more than a drop off. That he had come in person did mean we could discuss the royal wedding – my current favourite subject. He hinted earlier that he had an inside line on who was getting the gig and I wanted to hear more about that. Especially since he seemed to think it was me.

The why of it explained, I said, "It's lovely to see you, Rudyard. It must be months since ..."

"The Romain wedding," he supplied. "That was almost six months ago. Time certainly flies."

Mindy had been waiting to get out, her door largely blocked by Rudyard as he stood between the cars. He stepped aside as she swivelled her legs around and stood up with sinewy grace.

Buster plopped onto the cobbles like a baked potato dropped from a height.

"*Hello,*" barked Buster. "*I'm Devil Dog. You might not recognise me as I was a mere ordinary dog the last time we saw each other. Now I am inhabited by the dark. I can tell you my origin story if you like.*" I made a mental note to stop him from watching Batman movies.

"You have the dress with you?" I asked. I was making my way to the office – there were things to do, and it was cool out. Cooler even than it had been now that the sun had set. My motion was intended to draw Rudyard in my direction, yet he went the opposite way, around to the boot of his Aston Martin, from where he withdrew a garment bag.

The bag was personalised – part of his range, and in it we would find the dress. With only one bride left to give it to, the choice now was simple at least and Donna was the one who claimed to have almost reached her goal weight. She might even fit into it.

I waited on the pavement until he locked his car and followed us, then held the door for him to go inside.

Justin and Philippe looked up to see who it was, and Justin stopped what he was doing the instant he saw our guest.

"Rudyard." They shook hands and Justin offered to take the dress, his arms out for the designer to lay the garment cover on.

To my surprise Rudyard almost snatched the dress away. He held it to his chest, crushing it I thought, despite the delicate nature of the garment. He twist-ed to find me.

"Is there somewhere I can hang this?" he asked. "I wish to inspect it before I hand it over. Also, I would like to know who it is going to be worn by."

He was being precious about his work – something I could understand and respect. However, I was not the only person in the room.

Mindy asked, "Why does it matter who it is going to?"

Rudyard's face fell, his expression aghast. "Because this is not just a dress, my dear girl, this is a work of art." To demonstrate his point, Rudyard walked across the room to the stairs, hooking the hanger through a piece of the open banister before delicately unzipping the garment bag.

In seconds, the dress was free, and one had to admit it was something spectacular.

Speaking to the room, but addressing me, Rudyard said, "Usually, I am commissioned to create a piece for an individual, tailoring the dress to fit the bride's figure. However, for the purposes of exhibitions, advertising, and in this case what I thought was going to be a magazine cover, I sometimes make dresses without an intended owner. That is how this dress came into being. It will be worn by a common person, by which I mean the bride is neither famous nor marrying someone famous. You will think me arrogant, but I know my dresses are the best in the world. The bride who wears this captures a piece of history on her wedding day, and that is to be treasured. I will send her a bouquet and a card to be received on the morning of her wedding – a special gift from me to ensure she fully understands how privileged she is. There will, as you know, be a photoshoot and a centre spread to be published after the wedding. That is why I need to know who the bride is. It is imperative we meet. I spoke to Annabelle ..." Rudyard bowed his head and crossed himself when he said her name. "Such a terrible waste. I cannot imagine who would have done such a thing to such a talented woman."

No one said anything. What could we possibly say?

The room was silent for a few seconds until Rudyard started speaking again.

"Well, as I was saying, I spoke with Annabelle more than a week ago to find out who the bride would be. She didn't know. She was running a competition. Did you know that?"

I met his question with a grim smile. "I found out today."

Rudyard shook his head in curious disbelief. "Most bizarre."

"It should please you to know, Rudyard that the pool of brides has dropped to one. I still need to speak with her, but I will be sure to pass on her details the moment I can confirm she isn't ..." I stopped myself because I had been about to reveal that she might be Annabelle's killer – it's not like I could rule it out yet, "... isn't going to back out or perhaps now doesn't want the dress."

"Doesn't want the dress?" Rudyard repeated my words like they were from a foreign language he was hearing for the first time.

I only said it so I wouldn't say the other thing about Donna possibly being Annabelle's killer.

"I'm sure she will," I tried a confident smile. "Don't worry about additional material though in case we have to let it out a touch or anything. Annabelle had plenty. I'm sure her assistant Clara can let us have some."

Rudyard had stopped moving, his facial muscles frozen until he blinked slowly.

"Let it out?" he questioned. "You mean the bride is a fatty?"

Mindy's eyes went as big as saucers. Philippe's too and when he gasped, I just knew he was going to say something. It was a mercy that Justin was standing close enough to clamp a hand over Philippe's mouth before he could challenge the famous designer.

Calmly and politely, I replied, "The probable recipient is a lady called Donna Moscovitch. She is tall and slender. Obtaining material to let the dress out is precautionary, Rudyard, nothing more." Okay, so I was lying a little bit. Donna is taller than me, but then so are most humans over the age of twelve, and she is slender depending on how one defines the term.

I would judge her to be a size eight, which is very much at the skinny end of the scale. If she was telling the truth about getting close to her goal weight – I hadn't asked what that was - then she might be a six now, or even a four. It is a long way from being a size zero, but letting the dress out a small amount would not ruin its lines, or the effect Rudyard intended to capture.

Rudyard puffed his cheeks out, looking relieved.

"Okay, Felicity. I trust you of course." He touched the dress, smoothing the fabric lovingly with the back of his fingers. Dragging himself away from the dress, he said, "Down to other business then, Felicity. We have a few things to discuss, I hope." Looking around, he asked, "Any chance of a coffee?"

Philippe jumped to it, making coffee for all with Mindy's help. Buster settled under my desk, content to catch up on some sleep while there were no supervillains to battle.

My office/ boutique is a double fronted house with a centrally set door and large box windows on the ground floor. Upon entering, one finds Justin to the left, and me almost straight ahead, both our desks set as far back as they can go to provide a sense of space.

In both windows are display items and very large images depicting weddings in the sun or the snow, each image selected for how brilliantly the photographer caught the moment.

To the right of the door, several elegant armchairs and a couch set around a low coffee table provided a lounge area for schmoozing clients and prospective clients. Rudyard and I settled there.

I discovered he didn't really have any information to reveal. He knew no more than me and what he had to say was based on conjecture, rumour, and hopeful guesswork. Nevertheless, it was nice to be able to chat with someone who was also hoping to score with this year's biggest wedding. It would be like receiving a mark of royal approval and any business associated with the event was going to do well in the aftermath.

Staying late to chat with Rudyard didn't bother me, I rarely leave the office on time, but when Philippe asked if there was anything else I needed him to stay for, Rudyard made a point of checking his watch.

"Sorry, Felicity, I'm keeping you late."

I smiled. "Think nothing of it. I won't be leaving anytime soon."

He chuckled in response. "Yes, that's the downside, isn't it? We have our own businesses, and we avoid working for anyone else only to discover we drive ourselves harder than any boss ever would."

He had that about right.

Getting to my feet I said, "Well, I lost a chunk of the day when I found Annabelle."

Rudyard's face froze. "You were the one who found her? Why didn't you say so, Felicity? That's so awful."

I shrugged. "Wrong place, wrong time. It's how I knew you were going to be delayed. I was in her shop when you left your voice message. You were right about the noisy announcers at the station. It was hard to make out what you were saying."

Rudyard blinked at me. Once. Twice. I waited for him to say something because it looked like he was trying to figure something out.

"Is everything all right?" I questioned.

He blinked again, biting his lip.

"You haven't listened to the voicemail message I sent you?"

I shook my head, glancing down at my phone where it sat on the coffee table.

"I saw no need. Was there anything special on it?"

"No. No, I just ... Sorry, I'm still reeling from learning you were the one to find poor Annabelle." He aimed an arm at the door to make me move that way as I was blocking his path. "I shall leave you to it then," he said. "I look forward to receiving your confirmation of the bride's name. I am sure she will look magnificent."

I walked over to the door, ready to shake his hand and see him out. I had to wait while he patted his pockets and picked his car keys off the coffee table.

"Rudyard," I called his name to get his attention and pointed to his right hand when he looked up. "Sorry, that's my phone, I believe."

He looked down at his hand.

"Oh, yes. Silly me. These things all look the same." He placed my phone back on the low table and made an exaggerated show of finding his own phone in a jacket pocket. "Here it is."

We air-kissed at the door and he made a point of shaking Mindy's hand, generously advising her to stick with me because I would lead her into the limelight.

"*Oi, down here,*" called Buster, holding up a paw for a high five. Rudyard clearly wasn't a dog person for he hadn't looked at Buster once and paid him no attention now.

We watched Mr Kipling's headlights reverse away from the windows and his taillights disappear around a bend. With him gone, and the shop once again populated only by my people, I explained to Justin and Philippe about the afternoon's events and how we needed to write off two whole weddings.

I hated cancelled weddings, just hated them. You do all the work to set the event up, and then have to do almost as much work to undo it. Deposits must be reclaimed where possible and quite often a certain amount of leverage and threat must be applied to get the client's money back. I take a minimal fee to cover my expenses, and could take more, but stating up front that you will keep their money no matter what happens doesn't secure the kind of clients I am targeting.

It was done though – I wasn't going back to Mary or Gertrude to beg them to change their minds. It felt like we were at the end of a very long day, but there was one thing I needed to do before I left.

Now that I had the dress, I was going to arrange getting Donna to visit for a fitting. She was thinner than she had been, but despite Rudyard's thoughts on the matter, I would have the dress let out rather than let the bride starve herself any longer.

"Mrs Philips? Is that you?" Donna snivelled into the phone. She was crying.

"Donna, is everything all right?"

"The police came to speak with me. I was at work," she sniffed. "They said Mrs Richards was murdered! Why didn't you tell me she was murdered? You said she died, but she was murdered! And she was wearing *my* dress when it happened!" she barely managed to get the words out, descending into a fit of sobbing. "*She* got to wear it, but I didn't!"

"Someone murdered her in it, Donna." She was railing about the injustice of a woman getting to put on a dress she believed was somehow hers. Did she really wish to trade places? I got that it was a beautiful dress, but how could a person covet it so deeply?

"I know," she wailed again. "I'm sorry. I'm being insensitive. Did you know her well, Felicity?" I almost got to answer, but was still thinking about what to say when Donna started talking again. "It's just that I have been starving myself for months. I was supposed to come to the shop this weekend for a fitting. I was sure it would fit this time." She sniffed deeply, releasing that awful shuddering sound one gets after prolonged crying. When she spoke again, it was with a trace of hope. "Do you really think you can get another dress? Annabelle said Rudyard Kipling only makes one copy of each dress."

Relieved that we had moved past the terrible news about Annabelle to arrive at the reason for my call, I said, "I already have it, Donna. That's why I'm calling."

"Really? You're not kidding? You've really, really got it?" She had gone from morose to jubilant in a heart-beat.

"I really have it. We need to fix a date for you to visit so we can try the fit."

"Tomorrow!" Apparently, she didn't need to check her diary. "It has to be tomorrow, Mrs Philips. I need to see it for myself."

She was the only bride I had left of the three I started with this morning. They weren't my only three, obviously, but they had been the next three on my planner. If Donna wanted to come to the shop tomorrow, I would accommodate her.

"That's fine," I replied, doing some mental calcula-tions and planning. "It will need to be as late in the day as possible though, Donna. I need to arrange for a dress fitter to attend at the same time. Don't worry, I know several."

"Can we say three o'clock?" Donna asked with a level of hope so high I could almost see it.

I figured three o'clock would give me enough time; I could make some calls this evening. I told Donna as much, begged her to feel at ease, and ended the call.

With that task complete, another one materialised. I wasn't done making calls yet.

QUIZZING ANOTHER SUSPECT

I got Mindy to stay behind with me when everyone else left. I needed her to call Clara again. I could have done it myself, but the two young women knew each other, and I figured she had to still be in shock from Annabelle's death.

The purpose for the call was two-fold. To start with, I really did want to get hold of the extra material Annabelle had for the dress. Annabelle only did some of her work at the shop in the High Street, a lot of it was done from another building where there was more space for the equipment – the buildings in Rochester High Street were built when everything, including humans were smaller.

If the police hadn't seized it or secured it to sift for evidence – I couldn't think why they would – then that was where I expected the material to be.

The second, quite obvious reason for making contact, was the bit about her being a suspect for the murder in my eyes. Would the police look at her for the crime? I didn't think it would even occur to them. Perhaps evidence would lead them in that direction, but was there any evidence to find?

"Hello?" Clara answered her phone with timidity. "Is that you, Mindy?"

"Yes. How are you doing, babes?" Mindy employed a kindly tone – we couldn't treat Clara as guilty until we knew she was. However, if we expected Clara to lament about Annabelle's death, we were to be disappointed.

"Is there any news from Mrs Philips on a new job for me?" Her response further cemented my worry that she might be behind the awful murder.

Speaking up, I said, "Hello, Clara. This is Felicity."

Caught out, she said, "Oh, sorry. I didn't realise I was on speaker phone."

Mindy lapsed into silence, letting me take over.

"That's okay. Please come by the shop in the morning so we can discuss your options over a cup of tea." I wanted to look into her eyes and ask a few questions that had nothing to do with future employment. "There's something else I need you to do before you get here though."

"Of course, anything."

"I need you to bring some of the material Annabelle had to let out the Kipling dress. Can you get hold of it?"

Mindy and I could both hear the curiosity in Clara's voice when she replied, "Yes. I've actually got some with me. Why do you need it?"

Her question came across as a little impertinent, but I let it go – I needed her to feel she could trust me and that I was on her side if I hoped to catch her with her guard down tomorrow.

I told her the truth. "Mr Kipling dropped off a replacement dress. If necessary, I will have it let out to fit one of the brides." I didn't bother to say that there was only one bride left in the running; it was a detail she didn't need to know.

From Clara's end there was no response.

"Clara?"

Her voice came back. "Sorry. Sorry, you caught me by surprise there. I thought Mr Kipling only made one of each dress?"

"So did I, but in truth he only sells one of each dress, he makes several for photographs and such."

"Wow, okay." It sounded like Clara was trying to wrap her head around the new information. I didn't think it was that big of a deal. "Where is it now, Mrs Philips? I ought to let the brides know."

"It's in my boutique," I replied with a frown. "Mr Kipling dropped it off not more than half an hour ago. Please do not contact any of the brides though, Clara. I must insist on this." Especially since two of them fired me today. "Is that understood?"

Reacting like a schoolgirl being told off, I got a rapid-fire, "Yes, Mrs Philips. Of course."

"So we'll see you in the morning with the fabric?"

Clara promised to arrive at nine o'clock as we opened. She sounded hopeful about my ability to find her new employment, but also quite distract-ed. I put the latter down to the events of the day – whether she was Annabelle's killer or the unwit-ting assistant, either event would have jarring con-sequences.

Phone call complete, Mindy slid her phone away and confirmed I didn't need her for anything more this evening.

"No, Mindy, go home. It's been a long and confusing day already. Perhaps tomorrow we will do better."

Hitching her handbag onto a shoulder and twirling a set of car keys around one index finger, she hit me with an encouraging smile.

"Tomorrow we can look at flights and stuff, yes? A wedding on a cruise ship sounds like just the remedy for all the negative stuff we've been wading through, Auntie."

She wasn't wrong about that.

I locked up after Mindy, waving her goodbye before I set off in a different direction. I was going home, back to my quiet village where there was a bath and a glass of cold wine waiting for me.

Had I known how things were going to go that evening, I probably would have stayed at work.

unexpected House Guests

B uster wanted his dinner. This is nothing unusual. He talked about it most of the way home, prattling on incessantly as his stomach gurgled. He bounded from the car and across the frontage of my property to get to the door whereupon he then had to wait for me to arrive with a key.

My cat, Amber, a beautiful ragdoll with long fur of cream and smoke, was in the bay window at the front of the house when I pulled up. It was one of her preferred spots because it gets the sun through ninety percent of the day, and she can observe people coming and going.

By the time I was out of the car she was gone, nothing but the curtain settling into place to show where she had been. She would be on the kitchen counter when I got there, waiting impatiently for her dinner too.

Buster's head slammed into the door the moment I turned the key, the impatient bulldog happy to ram his way through. His back end scurried through the widening gap, vanishing into the dark of the hallway as he ran to get to the kitchen.

"Hey, cat!" he called. *"I've been out solving murders with Felicity. What did you do with your day, you worthless, lazy hairball?"*

"Buster don't antagonise Amber. There's no need." I flicked on the hallway light and shut the front door.

Buster stopped in the kitchen doorway, turning around to look at me with his head on sideways.

"No need? Annoying Amber is my raison d'être. Without it, why even bother to wake up in the morning?"

Amber's voice echoed out of the darkness of the kitchen.

"You wish you could annoy me, bone breath, but you are nothing more than foul smelling gas and background

noise. You are so far beneath me I rarely even register that you are here."

Buster wasn't fooled for a moment. *"Ha! I'm out solving crimes and you can't handle it. I'm the one with the brains and that's why Felicity chooses me to accompany her. Devil Dog is her dark passenger, always there in the shadows waiting to bring justice to the wrong-doers."*

I flicked the kitchen light on, making a bee line for the refrigerator. Amber was on the countertop as expected, delicately inspecting a paw which she then licked and used to preen the fur behind her right ear. That she chose to give no response to Buster's taunting was precisely the right tactic because it drove him nuts.

He stood on his back paws, barking up at her using language I was not willing to listen to.

Putting down the white wine bottle before I'd even had a chance to get the top off, I hooked a hand into his collar.

"Go outside and run around in the garden for a bit, please, Buster. While you are out there, think about what sort of words are acceptable to use in this house. Amber is your housemate, and you are not to threaten to put landmines in her kitty litter tray."

Protesting, Buster went out the backdoor.

Amber jumped down to the tile to rub around my legs. *"Thank you, Felicity,"* she purred. *"You really should think about having him put to sleep. He's not stable at all. You would rest so much better at night if he was dead."*

I scooped her from the floor, holding her in front of my face though she refused to make eye contact.

"You are a horrible cat."

She twitched an eyebrow and snorted her amusement.

"You are strange, Felicity. Even for a human, I mean. I am the most elegant and wonderful thing in your entire life. Now, open a can of tuna and I shall do my best to forget your comment."

I gave her a quick hug, soothing my soul through contact with another living creature. Placing her back on the floor, I said, "You'll have cat food until you can learn to be nicer to Buster."

"Cat food!"

She could exclaim her disgust all she wanted. The pouch of premier kitty chow went into her fine porcelain bowl which I set on the countertop. Buster's food – he didn't care what went into his bowl and always ate it so fast that I doubted he even tasted it – went on the floor.

He was at the door when I opened it, careening across the tile, paws moving too fast for him to grip the low-friction surface. He slid into the metal bowl with a clang, spilling half.

I fetched a glass from a cupboard, poured a generous portion of the cold, white wine and wasted no time in taking my first sip (gulp).

When I turned around, Buster had finished his food and was chasing the bowl across the floor with his nose as he tried to get to an imagined morsel stuck to the underside.

Amber hadn't touched her dinner. She hadn't abandoned it either. This was an old game we had played before. Amber would eat her food, but was going to make a big show of how little it interested her and how disdainful she was with my selection.

When she saw me looking, she shot me a look of such disgust few creatures other than a cat could ever hope to replicate.

"Hey, cat," barked Buster. *"There were two dachshunds at the office today. Guess what their human does for a living?"* He knew Amber wasn't going to reply, so

continued to tell her all about the paranormal detective and the ghost they were attempting to catch. He got most of it wrong, but I left him to it, leaving the kitchen and my pets behind as I went to turn on my bath taps.

I would forage for food while the bath was filling with hot water. I don't eat much as a rule, it's just too much effort after a day at work to faff around making something just for me. It would be easy to stray into the ready meal aisle at the supermarket – I know they make some great meals these days, but I used to cook all the time when Archie was still alive and there is a sense of pride stopping me from throwing things into the microwave.

Besides, fresh produce is better for me. I did open a can of tuna, Amber giving me the stink eye when I added some mayonnaise to it, plus capers and scallions. Tomatoes, lettuce leaves, some chickpeas, pomegranate seeds and more all went into what proved to be a delicious and healthy bowl of salad.

Unable to shift the images of Annabelle that continued to fill my head, and constantly questioning what I could have done differently today to have achieved a better outcome, I chose to drown it all out with a second glass of wine and some loud music.

I was in the mood for something lively and selected *Duran Duran's* greatest hits, a throwback to my teenage years. While *Simon Le Bon* belted out *The Reflex*, I idly returned to youthful fantasies about the handsome lead singer as I shucked my clothes. Slipping a gown over my shoulders to keep me warm, I went to check on my bath.

The doorbell rang before I could get there. It rang again and again, the person outside pressing the button over and over.

Buster's booming bark came from behind me, the dog's post-dinner slumber disturbed by whoever was outside.

"Repel the intruders!" he snarled, running by me in the hallway – I learned to hug the walls long ago. He collided with the front door, rattling it in its frame with sufficient force for the person outside to stop pressing the bell.

Coming closer, I could see a vague shape illuminated by the light outside. They pressed the bell again. Were they desperately impatient, incredibly rude, or bleeding to death? It had to be one of those, and as I approached the front of my house, my pace unhurried because a crisis on their part did not need to invoke a panic on mine, Buster identified the person outside.

"*It's Mindy*," he told me with a snuffling snort of the air.

It made me frown. Mindy wouldn't ring my bell like that unless she was bleeding to death. I had been about to call out to see who it was, but changed my mind instantly. Hurrying to get the safety chain off, I then heard her speak, but she wasn't talking to me.

"Just give her a minute, will you, mum?"

Mum? Mindy was with her mother? My hands were on the safety chain but had stopped moving.

I called out, "Ginny?"

My older sister's voice snapped back with all the usual arrogance and unjustified superiority.

"Yes, Felicity, it's Ginny. Now open the door! It's cold out here."

Ginny had last visited my house in the nineties, and I had stopped bothering to invite her more than ten years ago. We didn't live very far apart, but she had never had any time for me when we were children, and that attitude didn't improve with age.

I fumbled with the catch, got the door open and had to step back because my sister was coming through the door whether I intended to invite her in or not.

I might have barred her entrance had I not been so shocked by the presence of a suitcase in each hand.

Buster's policy was a little different.

He barged past my legs, keen to greet the visitors – I was letting them in and that meant they were allowed to live. They might have food, you see.

"Hello. I don't know you. I'm Devil Dog. I need to sniff you."

"Oh, how horrid! Get away from me, you mangy mongrel." Ginny never had been one for dogs.

Buster parked his back end on the carpet. *"That's a bit harsh."*

Coming through the door behind her mother, Mindy didn't hold back on giving her opinion.

"Mum, Buster is a lovely dog, and I think you need to remember that this is Auntie Felicity's house, not yours."

I let them get inside mostly because I wanted to shut the door and stop the warmth escaping. Ginny dumped her suitcase unceremoniously and glared at me.

"Well?" she spat the word as a prompt to get me to do or say something. Right now the only thing I wanted to do was open the door and chuck her suitcases back outside.

"Well, what?" I replied with an equal measure of attitude.

Ginny had the advantage of being several inches taller than me, which she used now to great effect. Looking down with scornful judgement upon her face, she shook her head.

"Same old Felicity. You haven't had me at your house for years and when I turn up unexpectedly, you cannot even manage to welcome me or ask why I happen to be on your doorstep in the middle of the night with my suitcases."

Mindy sighed with exasperation. "Mum, I think you need to be a little bit friendlier than that."

My niece wasn't wrong, but I could hold my own against my only sibling.

"To start with, Ginny. You always had a reason to not come to my house. I gave up inviting you after being turned down or ignored for a decade. Secondly, it's early evening, not the middle of the night, and as for your reason for being here, I think it rather obvious from your suitcases that your long-suffering husband finally decided he'd had enough and kicked you to the kerb."

Okay, so the last bit was harsh, but after more than five decades of ill-treatment, can you blame me?

Ginny reacted as if slapped, making a big show of gasping and looking shocked at my insult. I raised one eyebrow.

"Can we address the comment about me being a mongrel?" Buster asked.

"Why?" asked Amber, sauntering out of the kitchen to see what was happening. *"Calling you a mongrel is a compliment. I have much worse words for you."*

Seeing that she was losing, Ginny switched tactics, trying the waterworks instead.

"Shane kicked me out!"

"No, he didn't, Mum. Dad said you needed to get a job and called you lazy. Leaving was your idea."

Ginny ignored her daughter and wailed, "He's gone quite mad. He cancelled all my credit cards for heaven's sake."

Mindy groaned. "Because you spent twelve grand on a new couch, Mum."

Sensing that her feeble attempt to getting sympathy through pretending to cry wasn't working, Ginny shot her daughter a hard glare.

"I'm the homemaker, Mindy. It's always been me who was shackled with making the house look nice. I haven't done anything that is different to what I have been doing for thirty years. I'm the victim here. Whose side are you on?"

Mindy looked my way with a 'what-am-I-supposed-to-do' look.

Frowning just a touch, I asked my niece, "Why are you here? Why didn't you stay at home with your dad?" I was surprised she had accompanied her mother in abandoning her house and all her home comforts. Also, if she had stayed put, maybe Ginny would be more inclined to return. I could let Ginny in – it was the decent thing to do, but I didn't want her staying.

Mindy pulled a face and I found out why a moment later when she said, "I know the two of you don't get along. I am here to stop mum from driving you nuts."

Ginny jumped to a defensive posture.

"Excuse me, young lady."

Remembering my bath, I started back down the hallway, talking over my shoulder.

"Mindy is right, Ginny. If you want a room for the night while you think things over, mine is the first on the left. Feel free to pick whichever of the others you like." I had four bedrooms, the house bought when Archie and I hoped to fill it with children. The kids never came, and the rooms, rather than be left empty, became guest bedrooms. There were two made up with double beds for no good reason at all.

Ginny called after me. "Where are you going, Felicity? Don't you want to know what happened?"

"I have a bath running. We can talk later." I stopped in my bedroom to grab my glass of wine, then locked the bathroom door and my sister's muttering outside. I'll admit I was tempted to rescue the rest of the bottle, partly so Ginny wouldn't find it, but had already seen Mary Challis put away a bottle to herself – I didn't want to find myself in the state we left her.

Taking my phone, I sent Mindy a text message in which I asked her for the highlights of her parent's marriage going up in smoke.

I would get a full report from her while I soaked away some of my troubles, but just as I was slipping off my robe, the steam-filled air already pushing welcome heat into my skin, the doorbell rang again.

Mindy shouted, "I'll get it," but I was suspicious enough to withdraw the toes that had just entered the bubble coated surface of my bath.

I don't get a lot of visitors and unexpected visitors occur even less frequently. My sister turning up out of the blue was strange enough, but who could be arriving so soon afterwards. Was it my brother-in-law, Shane, here to patch things up? I wouldn't claim to know him well, but the man I thought I knew wasn't going to back down to Ginny just because she chose to act ridiculously.

There were muffled voices echoing through from the hall and the sound of the front door closing. I could make out Mindy's voice – the cadence and pitch easily recognisable even if I could not hear her words.

The second voice belonged to a man.

"Vince! Vince, Vince, Vince, Vince. Vince is here? Do you have a pig's ear in your pocket? I know you do. I can smell it!" Buster's excitement filled my head.

Somewhat needlessly now, Mindy announced, "Vince is here," with a knock on the bathroom door to get my attention.

"I have information about your bride, Gertrude Blithe-Leatham," he called out. "Shall I come in?"

He tried the handle, causing an expletive to exit my mouth as I shot around to check if I had locked the door. I live alone so locking the bathroom door isn't something I ever bother to do.

Outside, Vince was chuckling – he hadn't intended to barge in, he only wanted to generate a reaction from me.

Cursing him under my breath, and with a longing look at my bath, I stuffed my arms back into my robe. I made sure to draw the belt tight and double knotted it just in case – I didn't want to accidentally show Vince anything that he might like to see.

Harrumphing to myself, I opened the bathroom door, a cloud of steam billowing out to fill the corridor outside.

"Mr Slater." I heard a crunch and looked to my right to find Buster sitting on the door mat with his front paws pinning a pig's ear in place while he devoured it.

"Darling you are glowing this evening."

Ginny appeared in the hallway, leaving her bedroom to curl her lip in disgust.

"Who's this creep?" she asked, and though it wouldn't happen very often, I had to agree with her assessment.

As if nothing had been said, Vince produced a phone from his pocket.

"I'm sure you remember that I cloned Gertrude's phone. I had a look through the contents and ... well, I believe you will be grateful I chose to pop over."

Sighing, I gave a last forlorn look at my bath, and caught my sister's eye.

"There's a fresh bath going to waste if you want it."

Ginny, unable to simply say 'thank you' had to peer around the bathroom door suspiciously to see if she approved first. If she said there were too many bubbles or complained about the thread count of my towels, I would happily drown her in it.

Not bothering to wait for her answer, I took the phone from Vince's unresisting hand and stomped to my bedroom. Naturally, he attempted to follow.

Catching him as he tried to enter my bedroom, I pushed a hand against his chest and shut the door. He stuck a toe in the closing gap.

"I'm going to get dressed," I snapped. "Go to the kitchen and make yourself a cup of tea."

He withdrew his foot with an amused chuckle, whistling amiably to himself as he sauntered along my hallway. I shut the door just as he began talking to Amber.

Thoroughly curious, I dropped my robe and began fishing around in my drawers for clothes to put on, but did so one handed because I was trying to interrogate the cloned phone. I guess he cloned the chip and then put it into a new phone, but however he did it, I clearly had a copy of everything stored on Gertrude's memory chip.

There were text messages going back weeks along with photographs and emails.

Reading from the screen with the phone face up on my dressing table while I pulled on socks and a pair of slippers, I was about to join Vince in the kitchen when I caught sight of myself in the mirror. It was enough to make me groan.

I'd stripped off my makeup to get in the bath and that was how Vince got to see me. I knew I shouldn't care. In fact, I ought to be doing everything I can to put him off, but there was a vain part of me that didn't want to be seen looking tired and old at the end of the day no matter what the circumstances.

I huffed out a vexed breath and dropped onto my dressing table stool. Two minutes later, I had at least managed to hide the bags under my eyes and evened out a few of the wrinkles. My wild hair got yanked into a fast ponytail and I went to see Vince.

"What was it I was supposed to find on this phone, Mr Slater? It looks like a load of messages between Gertrude and a bunch of other people. None of it has anything to do with the dress or Annabelle Richards' murder."

Was he playing games with me again? I would not put it past him to visit me under false pretences.

He placed his steaming mug of tea back on the counter and swung his body around to reveal Amber smooching up to him.

She flicked her tail in my direction.

"I like this one, Felicity, but I have told you that already. Though it would normally count as a negative factor, the dog also likes him. You should let him move in."

I cocked an eyebrow. "Really, Vince? Bribing my pets again?"

Buster, sitting obediently at Vince's feet, twisted his head around to look at me.

"Come on, Felicity, isn't bribe just another word for love?"

Vince gave me his most innocent expression. "I have no idea what you are talking about, darling. I just happen to like your cat and dog." He stopped stroking Amber to fish around in his pockets, continuing to talk as he did. "Now, the point you make about Gertrude's phone is an interesting one."

I knew better than to ask, but I did it anyway.

"Why is that, Vince?"

He pulled his right hand from the depths of a coat pocket with a phone clasped between his meaty digits.

"Because Gertrude had two phones. One was in her handbag. The other was hidden in her glove compartment. It was almost fully charged though, so she uses it, but didn't want other people to see it. Why do you think that might be?"

I genuinely didn't know.

"Because she uses it for secret things?" I hazarded a guess.

Vince nodded. "Precisely that." He placed the phone on the kitchen counter and tapped the screen to activate it. "She has exactly one contact in it and has never made a phone call. There are no Apps downloaded to it, so she uses this to send messages to one person and one person only."

"Who?" I couldn't help myself; Vince annoys the heck out of me, but he knows his business as a P.I. and has a way of capturing my interest. Gertrude was up to no good, that much I had figured out for myself, but now we had her dealing with a secret contact! Was it a contract killer?

Vince gave himself a drum roll using two of his fat, sausage fingers on the edge of the countertop.

"No idea," he revealed with flamboyance. It was something of an anti-climax. "Gertrude must be erasing each message after she sends or receives them because the only information on the phone when I put the chip in was the number."

I frowned so hard I was squinting.

"Surely that also means she might have never messaged them at all."

He held up an index finger. "Aha. I said there was nothing when I put the chip in. A message came through not half an hour ago. I'm texting it to you now."

My phone pinged and he showed me the phone the message came from so I could be sure he had sent me the right thing. I understood why when I tried to read it.

"What is this?" I screwed up my face as I tried to decipher the code on the screen.

"Code." Vince waited for me to look up before he explained. "I've seen this sort of thing before, usually from married men having affairs and not wanting their wife to ever find out. They always do," he commented as an aside. "I'm not suggesting Gertrude is using it in the same manner, but there is a definite desire to ensure that should the phone ever be picked up by the wrong person, they will not be able to identify who sent the message nor understand what it means."

She was carrying an extra phone that was hidden in her car and she used it to speak in code with just one person. I had no idea what that meant, but it was deeply suspicious. I studied the single line of text, trying to make sense of it.

G1 – 1h – 4S – 556

"Have you tried calling the number?" I asked, not expecting to catch him out with something simple he might have overlooked.

He pointed to the phone. "Be my guest."

I twitched my hand, pausing to see if he was going to say something smart. When he didn't, I tapped the dial button. It connected to the number and rang, but no one answered.

"That's the same result I got," Vince admitted. "I tried it from different phones too, just to see if maybe the person would pick up, but their phone discipline is good."

I was trying to think of something we could do to decipher the code, but my thoughts were interrupted by my own phone suddenly going nuts.

I had plugged it in to the charger when I got home, and now it was dancing its way across the kitchen counter. The sound wasn't an incoming call or an alarm I had mistakenly set. Heck, I didn't know what it was.

Until I looked at my phone that is. Then the blood drained out of my face.

Meeting Vince's questioning eyes with my own horrified ones, I blurted, "Someone just broke into my office!"

BATTLEFIELD

Mindy appeared in the kitchen doorway. Like me she had shed her office clothes and was now wearing the figure-hugging sportswear I usually see her in.

"What's that?" she asked. "Did I just hear you say someone broke into the office?"

Vince grabbed my arm, holding it still so he could see my phone.

"You don't have video feed?"

I guess he was expecting to see the inside of my office displayed and a person sneaking through it to do whatever clandestine task they had planned. I hadn't sprung for the full package when I bought the security stuff though. I hadn't seen the need. There is no stock at the office unless one wished to steal brochures, flyers, or other promotional material. Why on earth would someone break into my office?

With a gasp, I blurted, "It's Primrose!" I was grabbing my handbag and yanking my arm away from Vince. "We have to go right now!"

It made perfect sense in my head. The evil, underhanded cow somehow knew I had hired investigators to trace the 'ghost' back to her and she was trying to recover the evidence before I could use it against her.

Clad in grey, baggy sportswear, I wasn't exactly dressed for an excursion, but I did at least have clothes on. As I ran for the front door, Buster hot on my heels, Mindy was hopping along behind me, putting her running shoes on.

Forced to wait while I put my coat on, Buster growled, *"Beware the night. It's Devil Dog time!"*

Ginny's voice drifted out from the bathroom. "What's going on?"

No one answered though, at least not right then. I was running for my car, Mindy with me and Buster already at the car door waiting to get in.

Vince shut the door behind me and ran to his car.

I don't know quite how fast I was going on the way from Twydhurst to Rochester, but Mindy was quiet the whole time. Watching through the car's windscreen, she used her left hand to hold the panic handle above her head and her right to keep Buster in place where he sat in the footwell between her legs.

The journey usually takes fifteen to twenty minutes depending on traffic. We did it in under ten.

I'm not sure where the calm thoughtfulness came from, but approaching my office I slowed down and turned off my lights. I could have parked right by the building, but I chose instead to stop around the corner. We had lost Vince somewhere en route when he got stuck behind a late evening double decker bus.

It wasn't something that concerned me – Mindy could apprehend Primrose if I had been fast enough to get here before she left.

Stupidly excited as usual, Buster bounded out of the passenger footwell and onto my lap the moment I stopped the car.

"Don't worry, ladies. Devil Dog is here to ensure your safety."

Mindy swung her door wide, stepping out and stretching her arms high above her head. By the time I got my door open and the daft oaf of a dog off my lap, she had her head gripped in both hands and was twisting it to unnatural angles.

"What are you doing?" I wanted to know, concerned she might rip her head clean from her own shoulders.

She let her head go and folded at the waist, hugging her legs like she was made of rubber.

"Limbering up," she mumbled.

Of course, years ago in my ballet days, I was every bit as flexible as my niece. Not so much anymore. Now I am a little older and I mostly ache.

Buster was doing his best to pull my arm off and he was right that we needed to get going if we hoped to catch Primrose.

There was no wailing alarm – I went for the budget option, remember – just a warning triggered on my phone. The street was therefore silent. Rochester High Street is a busy area, bars and restaurants drawing a crowd every night of the week. However, my little boutique is set away from the bulk of that.

Highly visible to passing trade, it nevertheless enjoys a spot set back from the road and at night it is both quiet and dark.

Mindy, Buster, and I slipped through an alleyway to reach the front of the building. It was dark, no lights on inside, and the front façade looked intact. There being only one other entrance unless a person scales a wall and climbs in through a window, I led Mindy to the back door.

It had been forced. Inside my head I was screaming at myself. I knew the building could be more secure, but getting a better door and a superior security system had never seemed like a priority. Honestly, it was one of those things that would occur to me once every few months and then be gone again because the phone rang with a client enquiry.

"The lock held, but they forced the hinges," Mindy observed, shining the light from her torch around the doorframe.

I would need a tradesperson out in the morning to replace or repair the damaged parts – my insurance would cover it, but there was little I could do now other than call the police to report it. Standing outside, I did precisely that, dialling three nines for the second time today.

They would send a patrol car to check on the building. To promote a swift response, I claimed the intruder was still inside.

With the call complete, I figured I probably ought to see if they were.

Taking a step inside, I called out. "Primrose, I know it's you. Come out now or my ninja niece will be forced to pound you."

The darkness ate my words, no reply returning. Not from inside, at least.

"Well, well, well," said a familiar voice. It came from behind us and made me, Mindy, and Buster jump.

Buster reacted as he always does by barking and running towards the danger.

Since the danger was Philippe's former boss, Henri, and a gaggle of his friends, I chose to let Buster's lead go.

"Go get 'em, Devil Dog!" My encouragement echoed across the cobbles, but the enthusiasm I felt was short lived.

I didn't exactly want Buster to cause arterial bleeding, but a bite here and there ought to deter Henri and his friends, I thought. They were at the back of my premises in the dark and thus clearly up to no good.

Their earlier threats came to mind – something about the premises being a fire hazard. Had they come here to set a fire?

Whatever the case, they came prepared, for as Buster ran at the nearest leg, a blanket appeared. In the moonlight, it looked like so much blackness until it covered him, and we heard his howl of panic.

By my side, Mindy raised her hands, forming loose fists and bent her knees to make her legs into springs.

"Right boys," she stepped forward. "Who wants to be first to get their butt kicked by a girl?"

Her comment drew a few chuckles, and I realised then just how many men we were facing. Coming closer, more than a dozen men emerged from the shadows. I could see more than one with a jerry can in their hands.

Standing front and centre, Henri said, "I warned you, Mrs Philips. I don't do losing. Philippe doesn't get to just walk away from me."

"What are you proposing to do?" I demanded, my voice affected by the adrenaline I felt and threatening to betray the fear I felt.

Buster yelped, *"Help! I can't find the door! How do I get out of this?"*

Henri paid no attention to the snarls emanating from the blanket.

"I think perhaps there's about to be a terrible fire at your office, Mrs Philips. Such a shame you and the young lady were working late upstairs. Do you know that severe bruising – say from taking a beating prior to being burned to death – doesn't show up in an autopsy? The tissue damage is too great from the intensity of the fire, you see?"

He was speaking in a matter-of-fact manner, his words and tone utterly terrifying.

One of the men next to him said, "Wait a second, Henri. No one said anything about killing people. We were going to set a small fire. That's what you said."

My previous experience with Mindy in dangerous situations is that she attacks first and asks questions later if anyone is still conscious. I took her lack of movement – she was still right by my side – to indicate that she thought the opposition force's numbers to be too great to overcome.

They were arguing among themselves now, but we needed to escape. I could run into the building and find a place to barricade, but would they then just light the fire? And what about Buster. He was under the blanket, the material wrapping around him as he fought to get free. He was trapped like a fish in a net. If I ran, what would become of him?

"The police are coming!" I blurted. "I called them before you showed up."

Henri's conversation stopped.

"Maybe you did," he replied with a shrug. "And maybe you are lying. Either way, it's time to get on with it. Killing you both wasn't the plan, but it meets the objective." Over his shoulder he said, "Anyone who is too squeamish or weak for this can just leave. Someone pick up the dog. He can roast too."

"Not so fast, gentlemen," commanded Vince as he strolled into the courtyard. His hands were at his sides, his posture relaxed, but I had seen him move before, seen him hit someone when he had to. They had stayed hit. "Are you ladies doing okay?" he asked.

"*I'm not!*" came Buster's muffled voice.

Henri had just been starting towards us, but paused at the unexpected arrival of a new player. He didn't pause for long though.

"Two victims, three victims ... makes no difference to me," he shrugged.

"How about four?" The new voice came from behind the men, their heads swivelling around to find a figure coming out of a crouch. He was standing on top of the wall at the back of the courtyard, silhouetted against the night sky.

From where we stood, he looked like nothing other than a black shape. If we were in Gotham City, his entrance would have put Batman to shame. Whispers were passing between Henri's men. They were becoming concerned about all the additional collateral and they had no idea who the new man was. In direct contrast, I knew exactly who had just entered the field of battle.

Someone in Henri's team said, "Henri, we need to get out of here."

Another new voice, this one coming from a pool of blackness to my right, asked, "Now?"

The black shape atop the wall said, "Yes, please, Ben."

What followed was hard to keep track of.

The black shape leapt down from the wall, vanishing into the darkness at the rear of the yard. As he did so, from my right, I heard what sounded like someone being hit in the face by a telegraph pole.

Making me jump, Mindy roared a berserker war cry and ran at Henri. Not to be outdone, Vince made sure to catch my eye so he could wink at me, then he took two fast paces and punched a man with gorgeous blonde hair in the jaw. The blow felled the blonde man like a tree before a lumberjack.

I was cowering in the back doorway to my office, unable to convince my feet to move until I spotted a blanket trying to run. The dark blob of material was barking and cursing.

"Let me out! Let me out! Devil Dog needs to dispense some justice!"

I want to say the fight lasted for ages – it felt that way at the time. However, running to grab the blanket and free Buster occurred about three seconds after I heard the first punch, and it was all over by the time I finally got him untangled.

Lights came on as people activated their phones.

Mindy shone her light to illuminate Big Ben.

"Hey," he shielded his eyes. "My night vision."

The giant man was standing in the middle of a pile of fallen men. They were groaning and complaining but none were trying to get up. Big Ben was counting them.

"Seven. I count seven. How many did you get, little man?" Tempest Michaels said something unrepeatable. "I'll be generous and call it one," Big Ben chuckled. "I believe the young lady got more than you."

Vince asked, "I take it you know these chaps, Felicity?"

Tempest stepped forward, going around someone who was lying face down and looked to be unconscious.

"Tempest Michaels," he offered his hand for Vince to shake.

Vince raised his eyebrows. "The paranormal guy? I've heard of you. Seen you on TV for that matter."

Mindy said, "Auntie has a ghost in the building. These chaps are figuring out who is behind it."

"It's Primrose Green, just as you suspected," supplied Tempest.

I performed a mental fist pump.

"The video camera is sending a signal to an IP address. We have a member of our team who is particularly good at hacking other people's systems. We haven't approached Mrs Green yet – I wanted to talk to you about your options first. We were just coming back from another job when we saw you outside your building."

"Then we saw all these fancy chaps with their lovely hair," added Big Ben. "Tempest didn't think the jerry cans were a good sign."

A set of headlights appeared in front of the office. We would not have seen them were it not for the back door still hanging open.

"The police are here," I murmured, wondering how I was going to explain the mess.

Flashlights came on a moment after the officers exited their car, the beams shining through the glass windows at the front.

Vince volunteered to get them, but I went with him. There was something I needed to say.

"Thank you for coming to help, Mr Slater." I found myself caught out by the need to be gracious and grateful, and the knowledge he would use it against me. "You really don't have to keep trying to rescue me."

"You forget something, my love," he replied without breaking stride. "I am in love with you. I know I do a bad job of containing my ardour; my heart always seems to beat really fast when you are around. However, I will be at your side, or in the wings waiting, until I get it right, or until you give me another chance, Felicity. What I will not do, is sit by and let something happen to you."

Now, why did he have to go and speak from the heart like that? One moment he is a rogue I want to douse with ice water, the next he spins some words together that make me want to kiss him.

Was it just a line? How could I ever know?

We rounded the corner at the front of the building and there was no time to discuss the matter further. Two flashlights swung our way.

The cops were not ones I had met before, but they knew Vince on sight. I'm not sure they believed our claim to have a small army of miscreants all banged up and in need of medical treatment in the rear courtyard, but they were swift to call for additional forces when we got there.

As you might imagine, we didn't get a lot done in the next couple of hours.

PLanninG a DawN RaID

More police arrived while one of the first two officers to arrive was conducting a search of my building. They insisted we were not to go inside until it was cleared by them.

Among the first of the reinforcements to pull up was DS Wishaw much to my surprise and pleasure.

"Mrs Philips," he greeted me. "You are having quite a day."

It was enough of an understatement to draw a weary smile from me.

The constable who went inside, reappeared from the dark.

"The building is clear," he announced. "It doesn't look like they have damaged anything."

His report came as a huge relief. My head had conjured all manner of terrible scenarios including vandalism and destruction and all my computers being wiped. Primrose would happily sink that low though I had told myself she wouldn't have come in person – she didn't do her own dirty work. For a moment, I had questioned if it might have been Henri who forced the back door but dismissed the notion – he would have set the fire and been long gone before we arrived.

"Can we go in now?" I checked with DS Wishaw.

He nodded and led the way, advancing along the back hallway as I followed flicking light switches.

My office had been invaded, but it looked untouched. Mindy went straight to a computer, bringing it to life with the click of the mouse.

"Computer looks fine," she reported, navigating to see if the files were still there.

I was about to check upstairs and turning toward them, I spotted the thing that was missing.

My heart stopped beating. I heard the choked cry of horror leave my mouth and was already wilting as spots danced before my eyes and tried to render me unconscious.

Someone caught me when I sagged against a wall and Mindy's voice penetrated the fog that my brain had become.

"Auntie, what is it? Are you okay? Auntie?"

I managed to burble, "The dress," one poorly controlled arm wafting vaguely in the direction of the stairs where it was very definitely no longer hanging. "Primrose took the dress."

Ten minutes later, with a cup of sweet tea inside me and my head bent down between my knees, I was feeling better able to function, if no less sick.

The Kipling dress had been stolen; that was what Primrose broke in for.

DS Wishaw was all official about it, wanting evidence and other inconvenient proof.

"I'm afraid you've given me nothing to go on, Mrs Philips," he said as kindly as he could.

When I started to tell DS Wishaw about the ghost a few minutes ago, Tempest had leaned in close to whisper in my ear that his practices in tracking the destination of the video signal might not be entirely legal. I couldn't reveal how I knew Primrose was up to stuff, but when the police detective was called away to supervise something outside, Tempest had another idea.

"The video camera across the street will have caught the thief in action. The quality of the footage might not be great given how dark it is, but I believe we will be able to tell if it was one person or a team, male or female."

I beamed from ear to ear. "Primrose will be undone by her own scheming plans!" Instantly invigorated, I wanted to raid her office right now - Tempest had already revealed that was the location they traced the IP address to.

Vince stepped in to calm me down.

"In the morning, Felicity, we can see if she will play ball. Getting caught breaking into her place will do you no good."

I didn't like it, but he had a point. If I got caught, Primrose would make sure I was prosecuted, and the repercussions could go way beyond me losing any hope of planning the royal wedding.

Grumpily, I said, "Okay, but I want to be there when she opens."

"We have Clara coming at nine," Mindy reminded me.

I muttered a bad word.

Vince asked, "Can you not postpone Clara?" making it sound like it was an obvious and easy thing to do.

I shook my head. "She might be the killer. She is up to something, taking backhanders from the brides, I think. If Annabelle caught her ..." I didn't need to paint a picture.

It was Mindy who proposed the solution.

"Auntie you are always in the office well ahead of opening time. Won't Primrose be the same?" She was dead on the money.

"We'll get there for eight. It will be better to be there before business hours anyway. There will be fewer people around."

The plan was set, and I felt good about it. I could accuse my biggest rival and I would have Tempest with me to prove his side of things.

DS Wishaw wandered back through the building to find me.

"That's the last of the fire starters loaded into the meat wagons." He looked around the room at the assembly of odd figures. Mindy wearing sports gear, me looking like I was about to start doing the housework. Vince had on a trim three-piece suit and the Blue Moon boys were dressed in casual office gear marred by the presence of dirt and probably blood in places. DS Wishaw skewed his lips to one side in thought. "You know, you lot really did a number on them. If they hadn't confirmed none of you employed weapons, I would be forced to make some precautionary arrests."

Big Ben smiled. "I am a weapon."

DS Wishaw had to tilt his head back to look up at Big Ben's big grin.

"Yes, well, your reputation is well- known, Mr Winters. Yours too, Mr Michaels." I thought the detective was going to say something cutting, but he reached out to offer Tempest his hand. "That's for Chief Inspector Quinn." They shook and Tempest dipped his head in acknowledgement.

I wasn't sure what he meant, but my brain wanted to tell me the police officer was thanking Tempest for punching the chief inspector.

"I wouldn't make a habit of it though," warned the detective sergeant, releasing Tempest's hand.

A small snort of amusement escaped Tempest's nose. "I wouldn't worry too much unless there are more around like him."

Wishaw muttered, "God forbid," and turned his attention back to me. "I need to return to the station, Mrs Philips. You would be amazed just how much paperwork I now have to fill in to process this lot."

Speaking quickly so I would not delay him too long, I fired off a question.

"Detective Sergeant, can I ask how you got on today? Do you believe you have identified Annabelle's killer?"

DS Wishaw paused. "I'm rather glad you brought that up, actually, Mrs Philips. You see, while I cannot discuss the facts of an ongoing investigation with civilians, I feel I must cover the subject of your interference." My cheeks coloured. "We were able to ascertain that the dress Annabelle Richards was wearing when she was killed had been sold to three different brides. There only being one dress, it forms an improbable, but nevertheless plausible motive for murder. Two of the three ladies in question reported they were approached by you today. It sounded very much like you have been conducting your own investigations. This is something I cannot strenuously enough advise against."

He waited to see if I would deny the charge or say something to defend myself before continuing.

"Ignoring the fact that one of the people you spoke to might well be guilty of murder and see fit to kill again to protect their secret ..."

Patricia's voice echoed in my head, "The first murder is always the hardest. After that the second and third victims prove to be much easier." She spoke with authority on the subject having repeatedly caught psycho murderers responsible for a trail of bodies.

"... you also ran the risk of ruining my investigation by tipping them off and giving them a chance to create alibi's and fabricate stories that might hold up well under scrutiny."

I was suitably told off, and I raised no defence.

"My apologies, Detective Sergeant. I meant no harm. I was just ... I wanted to get ahead of the impending PR disaster coming my way."

I got a sympathetic smile. "That I cannot help you with." He turned to go, but stopped before he had his back to us. "What I will say, is that all three brides have air-tight alibis. I will be investigating further, but I am casting my net wider." He dipped his head a final time. "Night, all," and was gone.

Left alone, the police departing, there was no good reason to stay at the office any later than we already had. It was bedtime, I still needed to get clean, and I hadn't managed to drink more than a mouthful of the wine I poured.

Tempest got to his feet, clapping Big Ben on one giant shoulder.

"I think that's enough for one night." A yawn split his face. My dogs will wonder where I have got to. Shall we meet here at 0730hrs?"

Mindy made a strange face. "Zero seven ... what?"

"Half past seven tomorrow morning," Tempest adjusted his clock from twenty-four hours to twelve.

I pushed off the chair and onto my feet too. "Yes, please. That would be most helpful. Thank you."

Mindy was muttering something about old people being weird and I think it was aimed at Tempest who was probably mid-thirties though he looked younger.

Outside the office, we split up, each heading our separate ways though Mindy was with me, of course, and Vince insisted on walking me back to my car. The police had been good enough to fix my back-door. It would need a professional to do a better job, but it was secure for the night at least.

"No goodnight kiss?" questioned Vince, hopefully.

Mindy rolled her eyes and got into my car, holding her door open for Buster to assume his position between her legs once more.

Despite myself, I found Vince's request funny. He was a terrible pirate with a shark-infested smile. I constantly felt that he was undressing me with his eyes, and he probably was, but beneath the carefully constructed veneer there were glimpses of a man with an open heart.

I just didn't know what to make of him.

Turning my face to one side, I pointed to a spot on my left cheekbone. He would either get this right and score a point, or he would do something silly. The former might cause me to open the door just a chink. The latter would most likely slam it shut forever.

Vince leaned in close enough that I got a whiff of his aftershave in my next breath and could feel the warmth of his skin. Getting it right for once, he delivered a light peck on my cheek and stepped back.

"Goodnight, darling. Shall I see you on the morrow?"

Opening my car door and pausing halfway in, I said, "We shall see."

Vince watched as we pulled away, Mindy staying quiet until we were around the corner. Then fiddling with her fingernails as if distracted and trying to figure out what to say. Eventually, she ventured her opinion.

"I know you said you didn't want to discuss sex, Auntie, but if you need any pointers ..."

Charmed, I'm Sure

M indy looked down the street, checking traffic and waiting for a delivery van to pass before she jogged across to join me outside my office. She had two travel cups of coffee and a small paper bag I knew would contain a Danish pastry.

I had risen early this morning imbued with a sense of purpose and a bellyful of righteous justice. I hadn't slept well, images of ghosts, murderous brides, and crazy makeup artist arsonists invaded my dreams, but I put the early start to good use by reading notes Patricia Fisher had emailed to me during the night.

The cruise wedding, as we were now calling it, was indeed to be a lavish affair. A lot of the detail was taken care of: venue, catering, person to conduct the ceremony itself ... the ship was a place where couples often got married. It made my task simpler, but there were a few special requests that looked set to prove tricky.

Not least of them was the bride's hope that her favourite rap star, a young person called Special K, would host the party, and provide music. I'd never heard of the young gentleman (I had to ask Mindy if Special K was a boy or a girl), and learned he was currently the fastest selling artist of the year.

Is it bad that I stopped listening to popular music in 1989? It all got a bit weird after that for me and the boy bands were precisely that all of a sudden. Not heart throb material at all, but someone whose nose I might feel inclined to wipe.

I would get on with attempting to contact Special K's people later. Right now, I was girding my loins for some overdue smackdown on Primrose. Actually, I wasn't too sure what smackdown was – it was what Mindy told her mum we were doing this morning before we left the house. It sounded good though ... really captured the emotion I felt.

A rumbling exhaust note coming from around the corner turned out to be a giant, black four by four utility vehicle. Tricked out with extra wide wheels, a body kit, snorkel, roof bar lights and more, it was driven by Big Ben, who waved cheerily when he saw me looking.

Mindy said, "Wow."

It was quite the urban cruiser.

From the opposite direction came Tempest. Bearing the same to-go cups from the same coffee shop, he was negotiating his arms to get one cup to his lips while not dropping the other and all the while being towed along by his pair of dachshunds.

Buster started going nuts.

"Yay! It's the sausage dogs again! These guys are so funny."

Checking there was no one in earshot other than Mindy who knew about my 'special skill' I hissed at him, "Why? What do they do?"

Buster looked up at me, his little piggy tail whizzing back and forth still.

"Well, Bull, that's the thinner one on the left, he talks about the world as if he plans to run it one day. I've met dogs like that before. You see, we all recognise that humans shouldn't be allowed to run the planet ..."

"Wait a second," I interrupted him. "Why ever not?"

Buster shot me an incredulous look. *"Are you kidding right now? For a start if dogs ran the world things would actually get done. Humans vote another bunch of humans to talk about things and not really make any decisions. What do you call those people again?"*

"Politicians," I supplied.

"Right, Politicians. You have made a mess of the planet, you rush about all over the place never taking enough time to get in really good naps ... honestly, if humans would just sleep more the world would be a better place."

"Okay." I spoke over him again before he really got going on the subject. "Bull the dachshund wants to rule the world. What about the other one?" I knew Tempest had given me their names, but I could not recall the second one now.

"That's Dozer. He's ... um. He's kind of not very bright."

This was the opinion I got from a dog who would regularly fall over when he tried to scratch his ears.

I ended our conversation just as Tempest came closer and Big Ben jumped down from the cab of his truck. We stood in the street looking at each other expectantly for a moment. Everyone was waiting for someone else to say something.

"Shall we go?" I suggested.

Primrose has an office in West Malling, a fifteen-minute drive from Rochester. It took us twenty, just due to the weight of early morning traffic, but we got there before businesses were open for the day and found a parking space right out front. Not only that, I spotted one of the people who work for her, a young woman whose name I believed to be Robyn.

Quickly suggesting a plan, I left Buster in the car much to his upset.

"Sorry, Buster," I gave his ears a scratch. "I don't think you can help with this particular task. There will be a chance to prove your worth later, I'm sure."

We got out of the car with me hidden behind Big Ben - he is big enough to hide me completely which was good because Robyn was bound to recognise me. I couldn't predict how she would react – my rivalry with Primrose was well known by everyone, so I was staying out of sight.

The moment Robyn activated the door to Primrose's boutique, Big Ben called her name.

"Robyn!"

Thankfully my memory hadn't let us down and upon hearing her name she paused, half in and half out of the door. Big Ben jogged forward, supposedly dazzling her with his smile, which Tempest confirmed worked on ninety-nine percent of women.

Mindy glanced at me for my opinion at the time, but I chose to remain tight-lipped.

Whatever the case, it did the trick, Robyn smiling back at Tempest's oversized friend and holding the door until he got to her.

"Um, do I know you?" Robyn asked with unabashed curiosity.

I was right behind Big Ben and heard his reply.

"Not yet, Angel. Let's fix that over drinks tonight before we get down to it."

I would have found something to whack him with had he, or any man, attempted such a line on me, but Robyn gasped and then giggled playfully.

Big Ben took her hand and twirled her, taking her away from the door as he leaned in to kiss her and she folded into his arms like a piece of damp tissue.

I went straight through the still open door, Tempest hot on my heels and pushing Mindy in front of him. Mindy was staring at Robyn and Big Ben, attempting to fathom out what had just occurred if I was reading the expression on her face correctly.

The side door we came in through – the main entrance was still locked as it was more than an hour until they would open – led to a short corridor and then into the main office.

I strolled in confidently, Tempest and Mindy fanning out on either side of me.

It took a two-count before Primrose looked up from what she was doing. Our eyes locked, I smiled, and she went ballistic.

"Felicity Philips! What the devil are you doing in my office? How did you even get in here? Get out now or I'm calling the police!"

On cue, though we had not rehearsed or even discussed it, Tempest Michaels dropped the little radio thingy onto a table next to him. It made a loud clunk. Everyone in the room was already looking our way, silently watching to see what might happen next when Tempest followed the radio with the camera Primrose had fitted across the street.

"I believe these are yours, Primrose," I said with a pleasant smile. "I'm just returning them. Did you really think you could scare me out of my office with a ghost?"

A smile flitted across her face, and I think she almost claimed that was exactly what happened on several occasions when she caught herself and quickly changed her expression.

"I have no idea what you are talking about."

Tempest took over. "We traced the signal from the camera to an IP address in this office. I can easily locate the computer it originated from if you like. You have been illegally spying on Mrs Philips's premises which under public statute four one seven, which pertains to invasion of privacy, is punishable by a fine not to exceed fifty thousand pounds and a custodial sentence of up to six months."

I had no idea if anything Tempest just said was even real or whether he was making it up on the spot and clearly Primrose didn't either because the colour was draining from her face.

When she next spoke, I knew we had her.

"What do you want?"

I smiled deeply and honestly. "Shall we speak in your office?"

"Just you," she insisted.

I laughed in her face. "I don't think so, Primrose." Not waiting for her to think of a new proposal, I walked to the back of the room and into her private office – easy to spot because it had her name on the door – and settled into one of the comfy chairs I found.

Tempest and Mindy followed.

I called out, "Come along Primrose. We both have other tasks planned for our days, I'm sure."

Her cheeks were flushed with anger when she arrived at her door, marching in with purposeful strides and shutting the door with force once she was inside.

The door opened again a heartbeat later, Big Ben sticking his head around the frame. There was a trace of lipstick – the same shade Robyn had been wearing – smeared on his cheek and he had a flushed look to his skin like he had just been engaged in strenuous exercise. I chose not to think too hard about what that might have been.

"Is that all of you," demanded Primrose, "or are there more to come?"

She was trying to be clever, and I wasn't going to stand for it.

"You obnoxious cow! How dare you spy on me? Fitting cameras across the street and putting devices down my chimney. What is wrong with your brain that you think these are acceptable things to do?"

Primrose sat in her big office chair, using her desk as a physical barrier.

"So what if I did? We both know you stole my hotel room key and broke into my room at the exhibition. And you stole my handbag. You might have managed to fool the idiots running security there and the police, but we both know the truth. I was getting my own back and you deserved it."

Tempest's eyes flared a little, but he didn't say anything.

Were my face not so flushed with anger already, I might have felt my cheeks colouring. Okay, so Primrose made a valid point – I had done those things, but only because she provoked me into doing so and because I thought she had killed someone.

Changing tack, I asked, "Did you break into my office last night and steal a Kipling dress?"

Primrose narrowed her eyes. "How did you get hold of a Kipling dress?"

It was an evasive answer, but had a big flaw in it.

"You know precisely how I got the dress, Primrose. You were spying on me, so you saw Rudyard deliver it yesterday."

Primrose tilted her head back and laughed, a tinkling, merry sound that made me want to staple her hand to the desk.

"You think I've been glued to the feed from that camera, do you? I have much better and more interesting things to do than to watch you do nothing very much in that drab office of yours." She was smiling at me, acting superior, and doing a better job of managing this situation than me.

She was keeping cool, and I felt like blowing my stack.

I took a breath and focussed on what I came here to achieve.

"I have no time to waste on ridiculous hate campaigns, Primrose. I am tired of your petty antics, and I am here to insist they stop. I'm not taking the matter of your spying any further because it will just be a boring distraction, but if I find you are interfering in my business again, I will do my best to make you sorry. Are we clear?"

Primrose held my gaze. "Perfectly. Now get out and don't come back."

I didn't move.

"There is the small matter of my office being robbed last night. You have video footage which may very well show the thief."

"And you would like me to give you that footage, I suppose." She waited for me to answer.

"Yes, Primrose. It seems like the very least that you can do in the circumstances."

"Well, no chance, Felicity. I don't care what you want to threaten me with. I don't think you have a civil case to bring against me or you would be doing it already. If you want the footage, go through the courts, and prove it exists. Of course, it won't by then because I am going to erase it the moment you leave my building."

My word she is a spiteful cow.

I sucked in a fresh breath to tell her exactly what I thought, but Big Ben cut me off.

"I think this is where I can be of use," he remarked cryptically.

Tempest got to his feet. "We'll wait outside then."

I hadn't moved and couldn't figure out what was going on.

Big Ben grabbed the bottom of his sweatshirt and pulled the garment over his head. Now naked from the waist up, I could see that he was even leaner and more muscular than I might have imagined.

Mindy asked, "What's happening?"

She didn't get a reply, but I did give her a nudge to get up and moving. Tempest was at the door, waiting to go out, and Primrose was yet to take her eyes off Big Ben.

It was beyond weird, but when Big Ben left her office just a minute or so later, he had a CD in his hand and a smile on his face.

"Works every time," he claimed without explaining what it was that worked every time.

Mindy had a deep frown creasing her forehead.

"What just happened?"

Big Ben called over his shoulder as he walked back to the door we came in through. "I charmed her into giving me what I wanted?"

Mindy looked at me for answers. "I don't get it, Auntie. Some old guy ..."

Big Ben stopped dead in the hallway. "Old guy?"

Mindy offered him an apologetic face. "Dude you've got to be like ... in your thirties or something. How is it that you take off your shirt and Primrose suddenly hands over the footage she said she would never give us."

Big Ben backed up a step and leaned down to whisper something in Mindy's ear. I didn't hear what he said, but her face flushed deep red, and her eyes dilated. Also, it might have been my imagination, but she seemed to be almost panting when we got in the car.

Curiosity was making me want to know what the oversized, stupidly handsome man had whispered to my niece, but I was never going to ask.

We had to drive back to my office to find a device that would take the CD and play what was on it, but with a little whizzing of the playback to get to the right time, we all saw the thief step out of the shadows. In a shaft of moonlight coming through the front window of my building, a face I knew shocked me to my core.

SHOCKING NEWS

empest asked the obvious question.

"You know who that is?"

I was still staring at the screen in mute disbelief when Mindy answered him.

"That's Clara. She's the murdered dressmaker's assistant."

Why on earth would she break into my office and steal the dress? I couldn't make any sense of it. She was asking me for help getting a new job yesterday. I shot my arm out to check my watch: it was five to nine.

Was she about to walk through the door?

"Mindy?"

"Yes, Auntie?"

"Can you please call Clara and just ask if she is going to be on time this morning? Don't tip her off, just find out if she is still coming here."

Mindy took out her phone, but asked, "What are you going to do?"

I dug around in my handbag to find my own phone. "I'm going to call the police."

Tempest touched my shoulder.

"If there's nothing else we can help you with, Felicity …"

He and Big Ben were loitering now. They had found my ghost and solved the silly mystery in almost no time at all, seeing the job all the way through to confronting my tormentor. They hadn't even charged me for it, employing the barter system to perhaps engage my advice at some point in the future. They were good guys, and I wondered if I might ever need to call on them again.

"Of course." I put my phone down to shake Tempest's hand. "Thank you so much for helping me."

Tempest gave a nod of acknowledgment. "It was our pleasure. If you ever need us again …"

Buster said, "*Well, actually I've been thinking about that. Given my abilities as a crime fighter, I believe I should be given a place on your team. Bull and Dozer have many tales of doing battle and I am famous for taking down bad guys.*" He dropped his voice to a deep rasp – the voice he uses when he's pretending to be Devil Dog. "*They say the night fears me, and that when I bark bats within a half mile radius spontaneously implode.*"

I had decided long ago that it was a good thing no one else could understand him. Right now I was especially glad.

Tempest ruffled Buster's head and headed for the door. They went out just as Philippe was coming through it holding today's mail. Seeing him reminded me of Henri and all last night's drama. There was an obvious need to sit Philippe down and tell him all about it.

He waved a good morning, but he was looking past me to Mindy. She had been speaking to Clara while I was thanking the Blue Moon chaps, but now she had one hand over the phone and an uncertain look on her face.

"It's the police, Auntie."

Confused, I said, "No, I haven't called them yet." It was next on my task list.

Mindy shook her head. "No, Auntie. I'm talking to the police. It's that detective sergeant from last night again. He answered Clara's phone. She was knocked off her bicycle this morning. She's dead."

I couldn't come up with a response. What was I supposed to say in reply to her statement? I almost laughed; the situation so ridiculous it couldn't possibly be true.

In the end, I managed to croak, "Dead?"

Mindy offered me the phone, handing it over and stepping back a pace. She looked awful; upset obviously, but shocked too, like it had been the last thing she expected, and she wasn't sure how to process the news. As I lifted Mindy's phone to my left ear, Philippe came across the room to comfort her.

"Hello?" I mumbled "This is Felicity Philips."

"Mrs Philips." I recognised DS Wishaw's voice straight away. "I'm so terribly sorry to be the bearer of bad news. I heard your niece inform you, and I'm afraid it's true. It was a hit and run on the A228 at eight thirty-six this morning. It looks like she was on her way to the shop in the High Street, which is odd because her place of work is shut while we investigate. Were you close?"

I didn't answer his question, I had too many of my own. Also, my overactive guilty conscience was telling me Clara's death was somehow my fault – she wasn't on her way to work, she was coming to see me.

"How do you come to have her phone?" I mumbled.

"I am at the scene, Mrs Philips. I was in the area and on my way to work when the call came in. I wouldn't have answered, but I saw who was calling and wondered if this might not all connect to what happened to Mrs Richards. I'm not a fan of coincidence."

"Did anyone see the driver or the car?" A hit and run could be an accident, but just like DS Wishaw I didn't believe it was. Someone had run the poor girl down. She broke into my office last night and stole an expensive dress – I was going to have to report that, but I wanted to know why. Why did she need the dress so badly? Was it to do with whatever underhanded deal she had been doing with Gertrude?

"Just a kid out delivering papers," DS Wishaw sounded tired, and a little bit beaten down by the horror of Clara's 'accident'. "He didn't see the driver but described the car as something sporty. He also said it was a dark car and was two different colours."

"That's Gertrude's car!" I blurted, startling Philippe who let out a squeal of fright. "Gertrude Blithe-Leatham has a vintage Bentley. It's black with deep auburn swage lines running down each flank."

DS Wishaw shouted something to whoever was with him, coming back onto the phone moments later.

"Thank you, Mrs Philips. I need to follow that up. I will call you back later."

He was gone before I could say anything else, my chance to tell him about Clara's break in and the theft gone for now. I could call the station and make a report, but I wasn't sure what good it would do me.

With the line dead, I dropped my arm back to my side, still stunned by the news.

Clara was dead. It sounded impossible. How could she be dead? First Annabelle and now Clara. Who would be next?

The final question echoed in my ears, filling my head until I said it aloud.

"Who will be next?"

Mindy wiped a tear from her eye. "What do you mean Auntie?"

What did I mean?

"It's the dress," I murmured. "It's like it's cursed or something."

Philippe said, "A dress to die for."

Mindy and I both looked at him and he pointed across the room, following his hand to a table where he picked up this month's copy of *Bride and Groom*, the premier wedding magazine where I had a half page ad each month.

On the cover was a beautiful bride, the sun glistening behind her as she ran down an elegant staircase holding her groom's hand.

Beneath the picture was the caption 'Ten Dresses to Die For – this season's styles'.

Quietly, Philippe said, "I had a look through yesterday when it was quiet. Mr Kipling's dress is number two. It's the same dress."

I didn't like it, but I knew what I was going to do next.

"We have to go to Clara's house and see if the dress is there."

SPY CAT

My plan was met with looks of stunned disbelief. Did I really mean to go to Clara's house
and disturb her family in their time of grief?

Well, yes and no.

Justin arrived – he always got to the office after our
nine o'clock opening time because he had to drop
his kids off at a school a bunch of miles away. He
could keep flexible hours without it ever bothering
me. Mindy and Philippe could too for that matter –
we all put in plenty of time at the weekends when
the weddings happened.

He came in just as I was going out again, but I
stopped to explain about the back door and how he
needed to find someone to fix it properly. That ex-

planation included gently telling Philippe all about how Henri had tried to torch the place and was willing to do so with Mindy and me inside it.

He was shocked and horrified as one might imagine, but also relieved to hear that Henri and all his friends had been arrested. They were unlikely to bother him anytime soon.

When I was sure Philippe was okay, I moved on to report other news items such as the dress getting stolen, and of course about Clara.

Justin slumped into a chair when I finished. "My goodness."

That about summed it up.

I couldn't be sure which part of the utter bedlam surrounding our business operation shocked him most. For that matter, I wasn't sure which bit of it was troubling me the most either. On my part that was almost entirely because I refused to think about it. My focus was all on taking the next step.

Doing precisely that, and telling myself it would be good for both Justin and Philippe to be busy, I asked, "Can you or Philippe look at flights for me, please? It looks like I will be joining the cruise ship in Miami and coming back from New York." Mindy clapped her hands together with excitement, then remembered about Clara and went back to looking solemn. "Also, can you make sure whoever comes to fix the door does a good job. Also, I arranged to have Rita Daniels come over at three o'clock to fit Donna's dress. Can you let her know that's been postponed, please, Justin?" I wanted Justin to tackle that job because he knew her.

Justin made a note on a handy pad and asked, "How many seats do you need?"

I shot Philippe a sorry look. "Just two. Mindy and I will go." The former makeup artist looked crestfallen and didn't try to hide it. "Sorry, Philippe. I can't leave Justin here to run the place by himself. We have just lost two weddings and need to drum up some more interest as well as doing everything we can to make sure the ones we have run super smoothly."

Philippe nodded his understanding, but continued to look like a wounded puppy.

The matter settled, I left the office with Buster snuffling along in front of me. Mindy ran to catch up. I think she wanted to ask about the cruise wedding and when we were flying, but she didn't, thoughts of Clara no doubt swirling around her head to confuse her.

We took Mindy's car this time, her nimble Renault Clio Williams Supersport giving us more room than my convertible. We needed it because we were stopping off to collect an extra passenger.

"Explain again why I am being asked to do this?" demanded Amber, sitting on my lap and refusing to make eye contact as usual. She hadn't liked that I came home when she didn't expect me because I disturbed her mid-morning nap. In her words, she needed that nap so she would be well rested enough to power through her main nap of the day which ran from just before noon until I came home at dinner time.

From the backseat, Buster barked, *"Yeah, why can't I be the one to complete this mission? I volunteer for it. Especially if it is dangerous and there's a distinct chance I might have to fight some ninjas. Or bears,"* he added after a moment's thought. *"Or tigers. Tigers would be good. I quite fancy fighting a tiger."*

Amber yawned. *"Oh, do be quiet, dog. If you ever met a tiger, you would wet yourself in terror and run away. Except you run with all the speed and grace of a dead hippo, so the tiger would eat you before you got two yards."*

"You're thinking about Buster," Buster snapped a fast reply. *"He's my alter ego and made to look ineffective so*

that no one suspects Devil Dog's true identity. Devil Dog is double hard."

Amber sighed. *"You sleep on a memory foam mattress."*

"Yes, but I fight velociraptors in my dreams all night long."

Finally able to get a word in, I said, "Enough. No one is fighting a tiger."

Mindy twitched her eyes away from the road to look at me.

"Someone has to fight a tiger?"

I tend to forget that I am the only one who can hear my daft pets. I took a second to explain what had been said and got back to answering Amber's original question.

"It has to be you, Amber. I need you to sneak into their house and find Clara's room. Mindy and I will be at the front door talking to whoever answers it. You are going to look for a wedding dress. It is prob-ably inside a garment bag." I had to explain what a garment bag was and describe what it looked like.

Amber employed her thoroughly bored tone to agree to my request, promised to do her best, which did not fill me with a huge amount of hope, and promptly went to sleep.

"Cats are so lazy," muttered Buster. Less than a minute later, his gentle snoring reached my ears, and I turned my head to find him upside down and stretched across the backseat. His jowls had gathered around his eyebrows.

Getting an address for Clara was easy enough, Mindy consulted social media, asking a couple of her friends while keeping her death a secret. Clara still lived with her mum which wasn't a surprise given the price for a one-bedroom apartment these days.

The house was in Rainham, a large town on the way to the Island of Sheppey just off the east coast. Mindy's satnav took us straight there, and from the outside, there was no sign of the awful bereavement the people inside had to be feeling.

Once again, I questioned if this was the right thing to do. Waiting would cause me a pile of additional problems I really didn't need, not least of which was the task of telling Donna the dress I swore I had was now gone. Would she even believe me? Would she lose her rag and fire me like the other two?

Then there was Rudyard to consider. I would have to come clean and let him know I had lost his dress. Would he trust me to ever have another one? It had been stolen, it wasn't like I accidentally left it on a train, but the result was essentially the same.

There was also Clara's memory to consider. If I had to report the dress as stolen, the whole sordid truth would come out. She broke into my building and stole it. If there was a way to cover that up ... well, no good would come of exposing the truth now. If the dress was here, I would find a way to get it back.

First, I needed to get Amber inside the house.

"*It's cold out,*" she complained.

"You are a cat," I pointed out. "You have a fur coat and have many cousins who live in the wild. I am sure you can manage to survive for a few moments."

I was trying to get her out of the car, but she had her claws in my coat and wasn't letting go.

"*I want tuna for dinner,*" she insisted.

"Fine."

"*Not from a can, Felicity. I want a piece of tuna. A piece bigger than you think I can possibly hope to eat.*"

I huffed out a breath. How was it I was getting black-mailed by a cat?

"Fine, a large piece of tuna."

Still eyeing the pavement outside as if her paws might freeze to it, she shot off my lap when Buster stuck his head between the seats and barked right by her back end.

He laughed until I shut him in the car.

"Hey, what about me?"

"Sorry, Buster. You're going to have to sit this one out."

I joined Mindy, the two of us looking at Clara's house and feeling the same sense of trepidation. Forcing my feet into motion, I went through the garden gate, down the garden path, and up to the door on which I promptly knocked.

Amber, muttering under her breath, strolled around the side of the house and out of sight just as the door opened.

"Hello. Can I help you? Are you friends of Clara?" The person asking the questions was a kindly looking lady in her late sixties. "I'm Jean from next door," she informed us, answering the question before I needed to ask it.

"I'm Felicity. This is my niece, Mindy. We both knew Clara through work."

Jean showed us a sympathetic expression. "It's such a terrible business. I saw the police car when it pulled up earlier. I couldn't have guessed what they were doing here, but a young constable knocked on my door not five minutes later, asking if I could come around to look after Sophia – that's Clara's mum if you didn't know." She fell silent for a second, reflecting on her thoughts before saying. "Do you want to come in? Sorry, I'm nattering and it's cold out."

I hadn't thought through that we might get invited in and now faced with what to do, it felt strange to choose not to.

"*There are no open windows, Felicity,*" meowled Amber, appearing to my right again.

I stepped into the house as Jean backed away to let us.

"Close the door behind you, Mindy," I instructed, giving Jean the chance to turned around and lead us deeper into the house.

I glanced over my shoulder when Jean was facing the other way to see Amber hop over the doormat. She took a sharp left, running up the stairs with silent strides.

In the house's small living room, we found a crowd of people all looking morose and many still weeping. Cups of tea, some being drunk, others finished or abandoned, were all around.

Three girls, all looking very similar to Clara but older – her sisters, I guessed though I hadn't known she had any, were gathered around a woman sitting in the room's focal armchair. It faced the television and was clearly inhabited right now by Clara's mum.

Jean whispered to the eldest sister, indicating in our direction.

The lady detached herself from the group, coming across to see us. I didn't think I had ever felt more out of place in my entire life.

"Thank you so much for coming," she said with a tearful sniff. "I'm Sara, Clara's eldest sister. I'm afraid we are all still trying to accept it has happened. Jean said that you worked with Clara?"

I nodded. "I spoke to her just yesterday. She was coming to see me this morning at nine o'clock to discuss new job options. I know lots of other dressmakers who might have taken her on, you see?" I explained.

Sara looked confused by my statement.

"But she works with Annabelle Richards. She loved that job. Why was she leaving?"

Now I was confused. Hesitantly, I asked, "Don't you know? Annabelle was killed yesterday."

I thought I was speaking quietly, but I guess people were listening because Clara's mum shrieked, "What?"

Now all eyes in the room were on me and they were waiting for me to explain.

"Um. I'm sorry to be the one to tell you. I assumed Clara would have said something." *Not if she was the killer.* That thought stayed with me when I said, "Annabelle was murdered in her shop yesterday morning."

There were gasps from half the people in the room.

"Was my Clara murdered?" her mother demanded I answer. She was sitting forward in her chair now, her face still awash with tears.

I opened and closed my mouth several times, unable to figure out what I was supposed to say in response to such a question.

"*I found what you wanted me to find,*" announced Amber, strolling into the room to rub against my legs.

"Stop talking to other humans, you need to go shopping for tuna."

"Whose cat is that?" asked Sara.

"Um, mine," I replied apologetically.

Clara's mum reiterated her question. "Well, was my Clara murdered, or wasn't she? Who killed Annabelle and why did they then come after my daughter?" Having received no answer, Clara's mum was getting to her feet.

Sara asked, "Why did you bring your cat with you?"

"Why are you still talking to them, Felicity? You promised me tuna."

I was getting dizzy trying to keep track of the voices coming from so many different directions.

Doing my best to answer everyone, I said, "I have no idea who killed Annabelle or why. Likewise, I have no knowledge about what happened to Clara." Neither of those things were strictly true as I believed Gertrude was responsible for both deaths and was most likely being arrested at this very moment. "I'm sorry I brought my cat. I ..." I sagged and decided to just tell them the truth. "I think Clara has possession of a special designer wedding dress and that both her and Annabelle might have been targeted because of it."

I silenced the whole room. For two seconds. Then Clara's mum fainted and the people around me exploded into uproar.

It wasn't aimed at me per se. They were all arguing about how such a thing could happen, fussing around Clara's mum who was sort of conscious and burbling something unintelligible from her position on the carpet, and generally getting upset all over again.

Sara touched my arm.

"I think perhaps you should leave now." It wasn't a threat or a warning, just an observation.

However, it was spoken in a firm tone, and I didn't need to be asked twice. Heading for the door, I scooped Amber. I really wanted to get to Clara's room or wherever it was that Amber had found the dress, but couldn't see a way to do that without having to explain how I knew it was in the house.

Sara provided the solution. "Do you think the dress might be in Clara's room? I know she has several hanging in there. She brings ... used to bring, a lot of her work home. She would sit and stitch things by hand in front of the TV at night with mum."

Grasping the lifeline, I said, "Oh, I don't know. Maybe." I knew full well the dress was here somewhere.

Sara stopped at the bottom of the stairs.

"I think you should take it with you. If it is the reason why two people are dead, I certainly don't want it in my mother's house." She invited me to follow her as she started up the stairs, wanting me to identify which one it was.

At the end of a short hallway at the top of the stairs, Sara pushed open a door, the sight she revealed making my eyes bug out on stalks.

More News

On hangers hooked over the door of a wardrobe sat the Kipling dress. It was out of its garment hanger and on display, but that wasn't what shocked me. No, it was the exact replica of it on the next wardrobe door that took my breath away. There was a third one, we discovered and then a fourth on a tailor's dummy that was still being finished.

I put Amber down, much to her disgust.

"None of this appears to be getting me any closer to my tuna," she observed drily.

I wanted to reply, but Sara was standing right next to me, waiting for me to say something about the dresses.

Mindy squeezed into the room next to me. "How do we tell which of these is the real one?"

"Real one?" Sara expressed her confusion.

To answer Mindy, I said, "Rudyard stitches an embroidered label in the back." I was already moving, heading to the dress farthest from the door to check that one first. Mindy went to the nearest one, and we both drew a blank.

What we did find was labels.

"This one says Mary on it," Mindy held up a rectangle of brown cardboard that was tied to the neck of the hanger with a piece of string. The one I had was labelled, 'Donna'.

Mindy gripped the remaining dress, opening the top so we could both peer inside, but expecting to find this one was the real Kipling Original, I was disappointed to discover all three dresses were fakes. They were good, but they were fakes and the third one was labelled 'Gertrude'.

At least now I knew how it was that Clara had promised Gertrude the dress – she was making one for each of the brides. Looking more closely now, I could see they were different sizes. The one I had looked at first was the largest, which is to say it was still a modest, and well below average, size ten.

I had no idea Clara was so talented. My routine took me into Annabelle's shop once or twice a month, but I had never really had a conversation with her assistant. It was probably true that the most words we had ever exchanged was yesterday when she accused me of killing her boss.

She had been taking back handers and had broken into my office to steal the real dress when I foolishly told her I had one. Was she Annabelle's killer? If Gertrude had mowed her down with her car, it seemed highly unlikely. In fact, I thought it more probable that Clara's underhanded activities had resulted in Annabelle's death.

Gertrude, for whatever reason, had killed Annabelle and then saw fit to kill Clara too. The police would figure it out, I didn't need to put any thought to it, which was a good thing because I needed to focus on distancing myself from the murderous bride.

"Is there something the matter?" asked Sara, politely questioning why I wasn't taking one of the dresses and leaving.

I bit my top lip for a second before explaining, "The real dress isn't here. These are fakes. Your sister was a very talented dressmaker."

Sara didn't seem to know what to make of that, and had no patience left to delve any deeper into the subject.

"Perhaps you should just take all three. Do you have a business card? I just want them out of mum's house, but if Clara is due money for them ..."

"Of course." I produced a card from a pouch in my handbag. "I believe I know precisely who these dresses are for. I will ensure to investigate whether she had been paid in advance."

Sara's impatience was evident when she said, "It's quite all right, Felicity. I believe I can trust you," and ushered us toward the door.

Buster was pleased to see us when we left the house, climbing up the inside of the driver's door and leaving slimy marks on the glass with his nose and his tongue.

Mindy, her arms loaded down with the three dresses, complained, "Ewww, Buster. That's gross."

I let him out, put Amber in, and took Buster for a walk up the road while Mindy carefully folded the wedding gowns into the boot of her car. It wasn't big enough for them, not really, but we couldn't put them on the backseat unless I had Buster between my legs in the front. I couldn't do that because Amber would annoy him or bat his nose or something and then they would fight, and Mindy would crash her car.

It was coming up on eleven o'clock and I wanted a coffee, the caffeine needed to fight against the fatigue I felt from getting too little sleep. We were going to head back to Rochester once I'd made sure Buster wouldn't decide he needed to relieve himself five minutes after we set off.

Buster sniffed a wall, adding his 'signature' once he'd deciphered whatever it smelled of. Thinking I could turn back now and get going – Mindy was in the car with the heater on and ready to set off - my phone rang.

I paused in place, fishing it from my handbag. The number displayed wasn't one I knew which usually meant it was a potential new customer.

"Felicity Philips, professional wedding planner to the stars. How may I help you?"

It wasn't a customer.

"Mrs Philips this is Detective Sergeant Wishaw again. I have more bad news, I'm afraid."

"Let me guess, Gertrude Blithe-Leatham evaded you and is on the run. You're calling to let me know in case she decides to target me because she found out somehow that I was in possession of the real Kipling dress she wants."

"Um, no, Mrs Philips. I'm sorry to have to inform you that Gertrude Blithe-Leatham is dead."

Just like when I heard about Clara, I very nearly laughed. How could Gertrude be dead?

I guessed she was overcome with remorse over the two murders she'd committed, or had sensed that she was going to get caught and took her own life rather than go to jail.

My head began to go all swimmy and I had to put a hand out to steady myself on a nearby garden wall.

DS Wishaw was still talking. "Under any other circumstances I would be keeping this information secret, but I appear to have found your missing dress. At least I think it's the one that was stolen from your office last night. It sure looks like the one in the picture."

When he asked me to describe the stolen dress last night, Mindy had found a picture on the internet and sent it to his phone.

I managed to say, "Okay," as I tried to get my head low enough for the sparkly lights to stop dancing. This was great news. Not the bit about Gertrude, which was awful. I mean the part about the dress. I had been dreading the call to Rudyard. He had a right to know, but that didn't mean he would be pleased by the news. As for calling Donna? Well, I had been giving serious consideration to letting Philippe do that and telling him it was on the job training.

"There's a series of messages between Miss Blithe-Leatham and Clara Montesquieu." I hadn't known her last name. "I believe Miss Montesquieu was selling the dress to Miss Blithe-Leatham. Also," DS Wishaw stopped talking to me for a second to speak to someone who was wherever he was. When he came back on the line a beat later, he picked up where he left off. "Also, I get the impression Miss Montesquieu was either involved in or directly responsible for the break-in and theft from your office last night."

"Why's that?" I felt like I ought to say something, and was beginning to feel less like I was going to throw up now.

"Well, there's the small fact that she had the dress. I know she had it because she messaged Miss Blithe-Leatham to confirm she did last night. The time of her first message was ten minutes after you stated the alarm went off at your office."

I could have told him I had a CD showing footage of Clara inside my office. I knew she was the thief, but I didn't want to get into how we came by the footage, not when Tempest had made it clear the police would not approve of his methods.

"It would help me if I could get one of these cases put to bed, Mrs Philips. Are you able to swing by and confirm this is the right dress?"

"Yes." How could I say anything else? "Oh, but where are you?" I was telling him I would travel to his location, but I had no idea where it was.

He was, of course, at Gertrude's house where, just like Clara's family, Gertrude's mother was probably distraught. It was an hour's drive from where we were, but if I could get the dress back and sort out Donna Moscovitch, then just maybe I could get this awful situation put behind me.

I made it back to the car, told Mindy that we had yet another change of plans, and settled into her car for the cross-country trek back to Tudely.

When I called Justin to stop the call to Rita Daniels, I discovered he'd already made it. I apologised, asking that he call her yet again and beg that she ignore the cancellation. I hadn't gotten around to calling Donna, so she was still coming. It would be a rush to get across the county, collect the dress from DS Wishaw at Gertrude's house, and then race back to the office to beat everyone there.

Nevertheless, I was determined to make like the swan and seem serene on the surface. My clients need never know how hard I was paddling beneath the water.

WRONG ABOUT EVERYTHING

In the car with Mindy driving, I had time on my hands to think. I had been talking to a killer yesterday and snooping around her car. What if Gertrude had seen me? Would she have been looking to kill me as well as Clara? If she thought I knew too much, would she have seen me as a loose end to be tidied neatly into a grave?

The thought made me shudder, not least because she would have viewed Mindy in the same light. I had been trying to prevent my business from attracting negative attention, it hadn't once occurred to me I might be endangering myself or anyone else.

But how was it that Gertrude had killed Annabelle? DS Wishaw told me she had an air-tight alibi – all the brides did; those were his words. She had to be the murderer though. It just didn't fit if someone else killed Annabelle. Not to my mind anyway.

Gertrude wanted the dress badly enough to have paid Clara ... was it a bribe instigated by Gertrude or had Clara been the one who was guilty of making the under-the-table offer.

It was another thing I doubted I would ever know for sure, and I had to accept that it didn't matter. I would ask DS Wishaw whether Gertrude's alibi still held water, but expected to hear that she had lied and convinced someone else to lie too. She killed Annabelle, killed Clara, and then killed herself.

It was terrible, but there was nothing I could do about it and it wasn't like I had played a part in the tragedy. The best thing I could do was collect the dress and attempt to make my one remaining bride a happy woman.

I was a little shocked to hear that was not how things would work out.

"No, the dress has to be processed, Mrs Philips," explained Detective Sergeant Wishaw. He was using a sympathetic tone, but also made it sound like I was being particularly dense.

"But you wanted me to come here to collect it?" I questioned where my understanding of the situation had gone wrong.

He cocked an eyebrow and shook his head. "I'm afraid you misheard me. I asked you to confirm it was *the* dress. If this is the one that was stolen from your office yesterday, you will get it back, but not before it has been catalogued. The case has to be processed and ... well, not necessarily closed, but it probably will be since the perpetrator is dead now."

"How long will that take?" I asked tentatively, hoping I could follow him back to the station, wait a half hour and still have the dress ready for Donna this afternoon.

He sucked on his cheek before hazarding, "Oh, not long. One, maybe two weeks."

"Two weeks? The wedding is in two weeks!"

I got a what-can-I-tell-you look in return. "I can try to expedite it," he suggested, but I could tell from his voice he wasn't hopeful.

This really placed me in a bind. I couldn't get the original Kipling dress my one remaining bride had been dieting so hard to fit in. She was coming to the office in just a few hours to meet Rita Daniels and be fitted.

That clearly wasn't going to happen as I wasn't getting the dress. There was no way I was going to call Donna and let her down at such short notice. I would just have to find a way to make it sound like we were using the fake dress as a prop so the real one would stay pristine.

I nodded to myself, questioning if the two weeks DS Wishaw estimated might become three or four. I would badger the police daily, doing my best to tread the line between keenly interested person needing their help and annoying pest who gets shuffled to the bottom of the deck.

We were in Gertrude's house just inside the lobby. I was allowed to go no further and had left Buster outside with Mindy so she could take him for a quick walk down the lane. Amber stayed in the car refusing to come out.

DS Wishaw looked at his watch.

"I'm afraid, Mrs Philips, that I really must be getting on. I'm sure you understand. With three murders to investigate now ..."

"Three?" I questioned, interrupting his flow. "I thought … didn't Gertrude commit suicide?"

The detective gave me a curious look. "Why would you think that, Mrs Philips?"

What was going on now? What had I missed?

"She killed Annabelle yesterday morning. Then she ran over Clara today, killing her with her car. Surely, she then took her life because she knew she was going to get caught or something. Are you saying she didn't commit suicide?"

He puffed out his cheeks slightly, studying me before responding. I got the impression he couldn't quite work out what to make of me.

"I am not aware of anyone ever successfully strangling themselves to death."

I blinked. "Gertrude was strangled?"

I got a nod, but DS Wishaw was already raising another key point. "I told you yesterday that Miss Blithe-Leatham had an alibi for Annabelle Richards' death. Do you not remember?"

"Of course I remember," I replied a little too frostily. "Sorry. I thought maybe she had been lying."

His eyebrows took a walk up his forehead. "Yes, well we like to actually investigate these things rather than take people's word for it. Miss Blithe-Leatham was at a hotel just outside Gatwick Airport with a gentleman. It took some time to track him down because he's a pilot and had already taken off on his next flight – it would seem they had an impromptu liaison ..."

The detective sergeant was still talking, but I was scrabbling around in my handbag to find my phone. I wanted to see the last message Vince sent me. The one with the odd code from Gertrude's secret phone.

G1 – 1h – 4S – 556

Staring at it now, the mystery of the numbers and letters faded away.

"They were at the four seasons," I murmured.

DS Wishaw stopped speaking mid-sentence, his expression now a tad suspicious.

"Yes. How could you possibly know that? What do you have in your hand, Mrs Philips?"

Caught out – the code in my hand had come from a phone Vince took from Gertrude's car. I was quite certain we were not allowed to do that, and fairly sure cloning someone's phone would also be considered a little dodgy in the eyes of the law.

Hastily concocting a lie, I said, "Ah, it's a code. I found it um … on a piece of paper. I suspected Gertrude you see. I thought perhaps she was doing something underhanded with Clara. So I was snooping. Sorry." I did my best to make myself look embarrassed by my admission which wasn't hard because my cheeks were glowing.

DS Wishaw manoeuvred himself to stand next to me and read the line of code.

"Gatwick Terminal One – One Hour – Four Seasons – Room 556." He exhaled a hard breath through his nose. "I saw this already, but on the phone that sent it. It correlates with the times they both gave for their liaison. You were right about Miss Montesquieu. We found a series of messages between her and Miss Blithe-Leatham. All to do with the dress, would you believe? They go back weeks. Miss Montesquieu was selling it under the table. The messages indicate she was making a fake to replace the real one believing her boss, Miss Richards, wouldn't notice. Miss Blithe-Leatham was getting the real one and Miss Montesquieu was going to make it fit her."

That answered my question about who instigated the deal. Not that it was really in any question given that Clara had three dresses made up for the different brides.

"We pulled the phone records for Miss Montesquieu and found she had also been in contact with the other two brides, trying to sell them the same dress. Quite how she planned to pull that off, I have no idea."

I knew. Clara had made perfect duplicates. Only a person who knew what to look for would ever tell the counterfeit from the genuine article. The police hadn't searched Clara's bedroom yet. Or they had but didn't know to view the dresses as a motive for murder.

I was still trying to bend my head around the facts as I now saw them.

I had to ask a qualifying question. "The man she was with, his name wasn't Eddie Thring, was it?"

"Her fiancé? No, I'm afraid it was not."

The detective confirmed what I already knew – Gertrude was having an affair in the run up to her wedding. She wasn't the first in history to do so, telling herself it was a final fling or perhaps planning to keep it up after the wedding anyway. In many ways I was glad to be free of the contract now – it had disaster written all over it.

I still didn't understand though. "If she didn't kill Annabelle who did? And why did Gertrude kill Clara?"

"She didn't, Auntie. Did she?" Mindy asked DS Wishaw to confirm. She had appeared at the door with Buster pulling on his lead to get inside the house. The door was open to allow for the constant foot traffic of police officers, the chaps from the coroner's office, and people in those one-piece, white, plastic forensic suits. "I've just been looking at her car," Mindy explained. "There's not a mark on it."

DS Wishaw gave a sad nod of his head. "No. It would appear to be the case that the killer is yet to be apprehended and has now killed three people. Another reason why I ought not to release the dress to you since it appears to be at the centre of all this."

Every theory I had concocted to explain the murders had been wrong. I hadn't even come close to working things out.

There was nothing left to keep me at Gertrude's house, and we still had a journey to get back to the office. It was time to go.

I gave the Kipling dress one last longing look – it was beautiful even if it had already cost three lives somehow. I think DS Wishaw was glad to see me go. Like he said: he had three murders to investigate.

COOTIES!

Arriving back at the office, Philippe was as excit-ed to see us as usual.

"Hey, Girlz! Ooh, what's with all the dresses?" he asked.

Both Mindy and I were carefully carrying the forged Kipling dresses into the shop, our arms full.

Justin looked up, rising to his feet to also help with the dresses and frowning with confusion.

"Rita was glad I called back," Justin let me know as he unburdened me. "She had no other work today. Why am I seeing more than one dress?"

Mindy said, "There's another in the car."

I blew out a frustrated breath.

"You'll remember I said I was on my way to collect the Kipling Original dress?"

Justin hung the dress I handed him on the banister for the staircase, spotted the label and read it, his lips mouthing 'Donna'.

He turned around to respond to me looking even more confused.

"Yes. That's what you said."

I held up my hand, my forefinger and thumb a quarter inch apart. Squinting at them I said, "I came this close to getting it. The police have to process it and we cannot have it back until they do."

"Will that be today?" he enquired just as hopefully as I had.

I shook my head. "Nope."

"Do I cancel Rita again?" Justin did not sound like he wanted to do that.

I shook my head again. "No, I have a plan." Backing toward the door, I said, "I'll be back in a minute. There's more yet."

"I'll go back for the other one, Auntie," Mindy announced. "I just really need to pee first." She hung the dress she held as carefully as she could alongside the one for Donna then ran to get to the restroom.

I needed to get Amber and Buster in from her car still, so crooking a finger at Philippe to get him to follow, I went back outside.

Philippe asked the same question Justin posed, "Where did these come from?"

I explained as best I could without going into too much detail, but he latched onto a single fact anyway.

"These come from a dead girl'z bedroom? Ewwww, they might have dead girl cooties!"

Buster had already run ahead and gone into the office, but Amber, riding from the car to my office in my arms, looked up at me. *What are cooties?*

Having not the faintest idea, I echoed her question. "Philippe what are cooties?"

Philippe dropped the dress over the first desk he came to – it happened to be Justin's who was forced to snatch at his mug of coffee to stop the dress landing in it. Philippe was doing a complicated shudder/dance and sweeping his hands over his arms as if trying to shift whatever a cootie was from his clothing.

"Ewwww. They're all over me," Philippe complained.

Frowning, Justin picked up the dress and placed it next to the other two.

"Cooties, Felicity," he explained in a patient manner, "are a fictitious childhood disease. Fictitious," he remarked with emphasis while looking at Philippe.

"Then why can I feel them?" Philippe continued to shudder/dance. "Ewww, cooties everywhere."

Mindy appeared through the door to the back hallway. "Whose got cooties?"

Behind her I caught a glimpse of the backdoor.

"Is that fixed?" I asked with a nod of my head in its direction.

Justin, out from behind his desk to offload the final dress from Philippe said, "Yes. The chap got here an hour after I called the security firm. It was repaired less than an hour after that. The bill is on your desk."

He turned back to the three dresses, hooking a thumb at them. "So what's the story behind these?"

I explained about Clara's unexpected talent for making copies and how we found them in her bedroom and were asked to take them away. That of course led to me telling him about Gertrude.

Justin could scarcely believe his ears. "Three dead? Three dead in less than twenty-four hours. Who could be behind it? Who stands to gain?"

Sadly, I didn't know the answer to that question, but Justin persisted.

"It has to be someone connected to the dress, surely?"

I sat at my desk, determined to focus on my work and not get bogged down with criminal investigations I couldn't do anything about. To wrap up the subject, I said, "It could still be one of the brides. I don't think it is. DS Wishaw assures me they all had sound alibis, but I don't know who that leaves."

Justin sucked some air between his teeth. "I know this will be a little controversial, but how about Rudyard Kipling himself?"

I shook my head. "I know what you mean, he's a little excitable when it comes to his dresses, but he was in London. I heard him calling Annabelle when I was in his office and the announcer at King's Cross was easy to make out in the background. There's no way he could have killed Annabelle and made it to London in time to place that call."

Mindy said, "It could still be someone from one of the families. Or even one of the grooms. Mary Challis's mum is a nutter, and Donna's dad looks like he might break arms for a living."

"It could be anyone," I concluded.

Justin, like me, ran out of steam. We had too many other things to focus on.

Philippe was kind enough to collect lunch from a sandwich shop along the street. It was already well after two and my stomach was protesting its emptiness. Donna was coming soon, so if we were going to eat, it had to be now.

Anticipating guests, I put both Buster and Amber upstairs. They could sleep there and be out of the way. They went into separate rooms, obviously.

Rita Daniels arrived just before three, bustling through the door. Behind her, Rita's daughter, a dressmaker in training, wheeled a large toolchest. I had seen the like before and knew it would contain all manner of thread, pins, buttons, sequins, swathes of silk and lace in numerous shades of white and cream, plus goodness knows what else.

The tools of a mobile dressmaker, ready to be dispatched to whatever wedding dress emergency might arise.

"Felicity." She crossed the room to air kiss both my cheeks. She looked around. "The bride is not here yet?"

I was about to reassure her that Donna was due to arrive at any moment when she appeared outside the windows. Passing from left to right, she had her father at her side. Behind them trailed a small entourage of mother, aunts, sisters and what appeared to be not one but two gay BFFs. It was going to be a squeeze getting them all in my office.

Mindy leaned in close to whisper, "See? He looks like a gangster."

I hadn't argued the first time, but she was right. He wore an expensive lambswool fitted suit. It was grey with a fine pinstripe, but the man's bulging muscles distorted the material showing off his powerful arms and legs. His neck was like a tree trunk and the tattoos creeping from his perfectly white cuffs and collar did nothing to dispel the notion that he might be a bad man.

In contrast, Donna was petite and the smallest she had ever been since I first met her almost six months ago to begin planning her big day.

They came through the door, Donna's father opening it and standing to the side to let her in first.

Thinking ahead, we had taken the dresses for Gertrude and Mary to a storeroom upstairs – having three on display would have required too much needless explanation.

Donna spotted the dress the moment she walked through the doors, her eyes flaring with excitement as she rushed across the room to get to it.

"Oh, thank goodness. When you said the original dress had been ruined, I thought all was lost. I know you said you knew the designer and could get another one, but I didn't want to get my hopes up. Oh, wow, this is amazing!"

While her father stood to one side, Donna's entourage fussed around her, all exclaiming their delight at the dress.

Mindy shot me an 'oops' look.

I sucked in a breath and delivered the news I couldn't really avoid.

"It's not the real dress."

Everyone in the shop froze.

Donna's father came a step closer to me, narrowing his eyes to look at me in a way that could only be described as silently threatening.

"What you mean, not real dress?" He demanded to know in his thick Russian accent.

A nervous laugh slipped from my lips.

"It's a prop. We don't want to handle the real one too much and this allows Donna to be fitted and content while preserving the real Kipling dress for the actual event."

Mr Moscovitch eyed me sceptically. So too Rita Daniels who knew I was spouting utter garbage.

Mercifully, Donna came to my rescue.

"Yeah, Dad. Don't you know anything?"

The besuited, tattooed brute settled into a relaxed posture once more and I did my best to not look like I was sweating. I was not used to lying to my clients.

In a back room, Donna was helped into the dress by her mother and a sister plus Rita. Clara had made it to the size Donna had been, delighting the bride who was now too skinny for it. There would need to be a flurry of activity to get the real dress fitted to her when (and if) I finally got it back from the police, but in just a little more than two weeks from now, Donna was going to be married in a dress few could ever afford. On top of that, she would get a feature spread in *Bride and Groom* magazine alongside Rudyard himself.

Her father didn't speak again the whole time he was in the building. When Philippe took him a cappuccino, all he got was a grunt of thanks. I couldn't help noticing how the coffee cup looked like a child's toy in Mr Moscovitch's hands.

They left just after four, the office feeling empty with their departure, and I cannot speak for anyone else, but I breathed a huge sigh of relief.

Rita gathered her things together, getting ready to depart too. She paused to say goodbye but had a question to pose first.

"What was all that about using the dress as a prop? And who made that by the way? It's very good, but I'm not sure Mr Kipling would approve."

Rita and I went back years. More than a decade for sure and I needed or rather wanted to keep her on my side. Despite that, I didn't want to go over the story yet again.

"Did you hear about Annabelle Richards?" I asked, by way of supplying an answer.

Rita frowned, not sure she wanted to believe me. "I did. It's a terrible thing. Are you telling me she made the replicas? I had no idea she was that good."

"It was her assistant." She wouldn't know about Clara yet – I doubted anyone did and I wasn't going to be the one to break the news. "It's a long story I would love to share with you some time. Perhaps we can get together for a drink in the coming weeks."

My suggestion got a smile at least. "That sounds great. Let me know when you can schedule me in; your diary is far busier than mine."

I walked her to the door, her daughter pushing the toolchest still. When they were out of sight, I let my shoulders slump in an exaggerated fashion.

"What a day. What a couple of days," I corrected my statement. "We lost two clients in the space of a few hours yesterday. Is that a record?" I asked Justin.

He gave me a wry smile. "I dare say it is. Still, you now have the space to easily accommodate that cruise ship wedding."

He wasn't wrong, and more than that, he had the right attitude. Yes, we had taken a knock, but we were going to bounce right back up onto our feet. The cancelled weddings weren't a complete loss anyway – we had been able to charge a minimal fee that was non-refundable.

It was a good teaching moment for Mindy if nothing else.

The door opening with a blast of cold air made me twist around to see who was there. Imagine my surprise to find Mary Challis coming into the building.

Working Late

She waved enthusiastically with her right hand, her excitement bubbling over. Her left hand gripped her fiancé's right, the two of them mutually bathing in the glow of their love.

"Hello, Mary. Hello Clarke," I was pleased to see them both and had a good idea why they were choosing to visit.

"Hi, Mrs Philips," Mary gushed. "Hi, everyone," she beamed at the room

Clarke released her hand and came forward to shake mine. "Mrs Philips I'm sure you can guess why we're here. We're rather hoping it's not too late for you to be our wedding planner."

"I know mum fired you," Mary was too anxious to keep her feet still and was all but vibrating as she got the words out, "but if it's not too late, we'd really like to engage you ourselves."

The smile teasing my cheeks contained a whole bunch of emotions. Happiness for Mary and Clarke was in there and so too was relief.

"I could not think of a thing I would rather do," I clapped my hands together gleefully. "We haven't had a chance to cancel any of the arrangements yet." With their wedding set to occur in just a few weeks, everything was booked and double checked. I cut my eyes to Justin, asking if he was about to tell me I had that wrong. He'd been here all day getting stuff done.

"There's nothing that cannot be hastily rearranged," he let me know.

"That's good. That's good," remarked Clarke, the big 'but' that was coming evident in his tone before he got to it. "But we are on a tighter budget now that Mary's mother is refusing to pay for anything, and we have both just quit our jobs."

I took them to our comfortable chairs, Philippe stepping in to offer them beverages as was our custom. With them seated comfortably, I dealt with the tricky subject of budget and what they could or should sacrifice or shift.

The flowers could be toned down, the string quartet at the reception went straight out the window as did the harpist set to be playing in the church entrance when guests were arriving. I was trimming money from my commission by helping them craft a cheaper wedding, but a lower budget wedding would net me more income than no wedding at all.

Better yet, I realised, Primrose wasn't getting either of the cancelled events. This time yesterday, I felt certain she had them both in the bag.

Justin announced his need to get going. He had put in a full day at the office – a rarity as that is not his purpose in the business. We all muck in to make it work, but my master of ceremonies would lose many weekends throughout the year so cherished each evening with his wife and children.

I wasn't going to stand in the way of that.

Philippe was spinning his wheels, hanging around because I was working, and doing his best to be useful. Mindy had admin tasks: mail shots, electronic marketing, and a bunch of other things to do that we hadn't gotten around to teaching Philippe yet, but when Mary and Clarke were ready to leave, I told both my assistants to head out too.

Philippe grabbed his bag before I had even finished telling him to go home, but Mindy was more reserved.

She asked, "You're planning to work late?"

I was settling behind my desk already and didn't look up when I replied.

"Yes, I feel utterly disorganised. I'm just going to spend an hour making sure I have the next month or so under control. Plus, we have a wedding on a cruise ship to plan."

"Bye, ladieeez!" Philippe called out as he left the building. "See you in the morning."

Mindy put her coat back on the peg in the corner.

"What can I do to help?"

I was going to say I couldn't think of anything I needed help with, but asked, "Can you get Amber and Buster, please?"

She took the stairs two at a time, running up them with athletic grace. Moments later, Buster charged down them, making a racket as he came. Amber didn't bother to walk down at all, she was in Mindy's arms, no doubt refusing to move from whatever spot she'd been in until my niece picked her up.

Amber looked right at me. "*I do not detect the scent of fresh line-caught tuna. Why is that?*"

Placing my cat on the floor Mindy asked, "Anything else?"

Tempting though it was to have someone for company, I didn't need her and would probably spend the next hour or so with my eyes staring at my screen as I made notes, checked things, and relieved some of the worry I felt. There was probably nothing to worry about, but that wouldn't stop me. Double checking everything would.

"You go home, Mindy. There's no reason for you to work late. I would like a bath when I get home though. I didn't get the one I ran last night," I reminded her. "So if you can let your mum know ..."

"Sure thing, Auntie."

Struck by a thought that had been banging around in my head for most of the day, I asked, "Do you think your mum will want to stay long?"

Mindy sniggered. "That I cannot say, Auntie. It's not the first time dad has kicked off about how little she does around the house. I don't blame him, but … well, you know my mum."

Yes, I did. She was stubborn as a mule, had an unjustifiably high opinion of herself, and refused to ever apologise. I found myself worried that if she stayed with me for too long, Shane might decide he was better off without her.

I picked up my phone, remembering that I had a responsibility to place a call to Rudyard.

"You should go," I expressed again. "Oh, but can you pick up a fresh tuna steak from the supermarket on your way home," I added. Amber was still staring at me.

"*One that is too big for me to possibly eat in one sitting*," Amber reminded me of her terms, and I translated them to Mindy.

Mindy slipped her coat over her shoulders, "Right. What if they haven't got any tuna?"

Amber narrowed her eyes. "*Then keep going to different shops until you find one that does*," she meowled with a sense of bored exasperation.

I said, "Just get whatever looks good." When Amber cleared her throat, I cut my eyes at her. "I'll make it taste nice and I'll get you tuna another day, okay?

Mindy isn't driving all over the local area trying to find you fresh tuna."

Dissatisfied with my response, Amber trotted back up the stairs with a flick of her tail to show her displeasure.

Mindy left and the office fell silent. I locked the front door for good practice, not that I expected anyone to come by this late in the day.

Settling at my desk once more, I dealt with the least attractive task on my list – that of letting Rudyard know my office had been robbed and his dress was now in the hands of the police. I wasn't sure what to expect, but a verbal high-five wasn't on the list.

With the phone ringing in my ear, I ran through a few opening sentences, but I didn't get to employ any because the phone went to voicemail.

I dabbed the red button to end the call and thought about whether to text instead. I decided against doing so, putting it on the list as a last resort if I couldn't get him in my next few attempts.

Placing the phone to one side with a plan to try again in a few minutes, I clicked the mouse on my computer and opened the file marked Mary Challis. I have always labelled my weddings using the bride's name. I'm not sure why, it's just what I did when I first started, and I've never seen a reason to change it.

Of course, back when I was cutting my teeth in this trade, there were no computers. Or rather, there were, but they were big, expensive, and complex, and I was happy with a hardbacked ledger.

How times have changed.

I typed up some notes from this afternoon's unexpected visit, changing details as agreed and doing what I could to bring Clarke and Mary's event in on budget. The final number was more than they said they could pay, and a more mercenary businessperson might have called them in for a second round of discussions, forcing them to choose a feature they wouldn't have.

I just reduced my fee. I would earn enough, and it wasn't like I needed the money. I already had everything I wanted.

When the file was complete, I sent a copy to the printer and got up to make myself a cup of tea. I had to step over Buster – he was on his back with his paws in the air and his jowls around his ears again. His snoring would drown out a jet engine.

Picking up my phone because I still needed to let Rudyard know about the dress, I saw the time and realised more than half an hour had slipped by.

He hadn't called back, which struck me as rather odd.

Flicking the kettle to boil, I placed my phone down so I could fish out a teabag and thumbed the button to call him again. Just as the screen changed, I noticed the little number next to the voicemail icon. Rudyard had called me yesterday not long after I found Annabelle. I'd missed the call and then ran into Henri and his goons. Then I had the thing with the Blue Moon boys and the day just got away from me.

The phone connected but Rudyard still didn't answer, and a sense of terrible dread crept over me.

The dress! It was all about the dress, and the killer had moved up the chain to strike at the man who had made it! Rudyard wasn't answering his phone because he was dead.

The call went to voicemail again, but this time I had no hesitation in jabbing the button to end the call. The kettle was getting excited, roiling steam shooting from the spout, but thoughts of tea were behind me.

Was I going to have to call the police to tip them off?

Poised with my fingers ready to tap the nine button three times, I stopped myself and pressed the button to connect me to voicemail instead. Would there be a clue in the message he left me? Could it be that this was all to do with something he was doing? Was the killer one of his rivals?

"*You have one new message.*" The electronic voice informed me.

The voicemail started playing, and Rudyard's voice echoed out of my phone. Was this the last time I would ever hear his voice?

"Felicity, hi, this is Rudyard Kipling. I'm at King's Cross Station about to board a train. Oh, you can probably hear that." His comment was referring to the announcer talking in the background. He carried on speaking, but I wasn't hearing his words, I was focused on what the announcer was saying.

"*Passenger Karen Woodruff please report to lost and found. That's passenger Karen Woodruff to lost and found.*"

I held my breath, waiting to hear what the announcer would say next. Rudyard was talking all the while, but I paid him no attention.

"The 1227 service to Newcastle is about to leave from platform two. Final boarding."

"... consequently, I've missed the chance to get to Rochester for our meeting. I'll call later to rearrange. We really need to talk about the royal wedding in the very near future," Rudyard prattled on. "I believe it is now very much a two-horse race."

I backed away from my phone, my hands coming up to my face in horror. Rudyard called me just a few minutes after he left the message on the answerphone in Annabelle's office. Just a few minutes, but the announcer's words were exactly the same ones I'd heard when he left the message for Annabelle.

The message ended and switched over to the machine again.

"Message ends. Press one to repeat, two to delete, three to save."

I jabbed the number three, saving the message because DS Wishaw was going to want to hear it. Rudyard had called me after he left the message for Annabelle, but the time displayed on her office phone was 1227.

It was after 1227 when he called me, and that meant the background noise I heard was a recording.

He faked it. I could only come up with one reason why he would.

The sound of the back door closing gave me a start. I had my phone in my hand and was ready to dial the police, but I couldn't convince my hands to move.

TYING OFF A LOOSE END

Buster snuffled and rolled onto his paws.

"Hmmm? Whassat? Is it dinner time?" he asked sleepily.

My eyes were glued to the door in the back wall of the office, telling myself I was hearing things. One second passed. Two.

Buster reached up with one back paw to scratch at an ear as he idly commented. *"Felicity, are you expecting a visitor?"*

I had just enough presence of mind to blurt, "It's Rudyard! He's the killer!" before Rudyard opened the door and walked in.

Buster needed no command to get moving. He even forwent his usual superhero trumpet call as he exploded into action.

His stubby legs scrambled for purchase, his claws digging into the thin carpet as he barked and lunged. I had almost sent both Amber and Buster home with Mindy, only keeping them with me because their company is comforting. Thank goodness I had because my dog was going to take down the homicidal maniac designer before Rudyard could add me to his list of victims.

Buster went for Rudyard's shins, leaping off the ground with his mouth open to sink in his teeth.

Rudyard nimbly sidestepped, avoiding Buster completely. With nothing to arrest his forward motion, I got to watch my dog ... my defender, sail through the open door and into the hallway beyond.

Rudyard slammed the door shut in a single motion and flicked the lock.

Unable to believe my eyes, I backed away. My breaths were coming in ragged lumps, adrenalin and fear driving my heartrate through the roof.

For no good reason at all, I squeaked, "How did you get in?"

Rudyard's eyes were hard, narrowed to slits as he stalked toward me, slowly and confidently.

"The key was in the backdoor, my dear. You should be less careless with your security."

The news stole my next breath, making me gasp. The workmen had left it set up ready for us, undoubtedly expecting us to find the keys when we locked up. But the back door was never used. I hadn't been through it in months until last night. It might have stayed unlocked forever had Rudyard not pointed out my omission.

Now was not the time to thank him though.

"I'm truly sorry, Felicity. If it's any consolation, I believe your death will be a severe loss to the wedding community. I was rooting for you to get the royal wedding contract."

"Consolation?" I choked on the word as it stuck in my throat. "How about if you just don't kill me?" I was eyeing the front door, wondering if I could get to it. I did a poor job of masking what I was doing.

Rudyard threw a chair out of his way, smashing it across the room with a ferocious swing and his tone changed.

A hard thud rattled the door from the hallway in its frame.

"I'm coming, Felicity!" Buster was trying to break through. It was one of those cheap interior doors made from thin fibre board. If I bought him enough time, Buster would create a hole.

Rudyard either didn't think Buster could get through the door or was planning to kill me before he could.

Making sure I had no possible route to either door, he said, "Like I said, Felicity, I'm truly sorry. I even tried to take your phone yesterday so I wouldn't have to come back and do this."

My mind flashed to a memory of him having my phone. I'd dismissed it at the time, assuming he'd thought it was his just like he said. Now that he was here to tie off his one remaining loose end, all the clues were revealing themselves. His car for a start.

When DS Wishaw told me the paperboy saw a sport two-tone car, I immediately fingered Gertrude. It never once occurred to me that Rudyard's Aston Martin could also fit the description. His car was dark grey with a deep red hood and the epitome of a modern sports car.

Rudyard came closer, forcing me to back away. Soon I would reach the wall and run out of room. I looked around for a weapon.

"It was an honest mistake, you see. How was I to know you would hear the message I left for the police to find at Annabelle's?" He came forward again.

I had my desk and a table between us. If he went over them to get to me or ran either way around, he would give me the chance I needed to get across the room and out of the door. He might tag me with an arm and be able to grab hold as I darted to safety, but it looked to be my best hope.

"I knew when you told me. I knew you would figure out I had faked the message if you listened to the one I sent you."

"Why?" I managed to blurt. "Why did you kill Annabelle? Why did you kill any of them?"

Buster's head hit the door with a resounding thunk.

Rudyard's expression hardened, changing from apologetic and sympathetic to angry and murderous.

"She was going to put a fat girl into my dress! She was letting it out! Do you know what my dresses are worth?"

I did actually, and it was staggering what some peo-ple would pay for a garment they would only wear once.

Buster's head hit the door again.

"It was a publicity stunt. I was going to give away a dress and do a big charity thing for an ordinary girl off the street. When my marketing team first suggested it, I scoffed. Then they landed the centre spread in *Bride and Groom*. You can't buy a centre spread in *Bride and Groom*! Do you know what that's worth? And Annabelle Richards was going to let my dress out to fit a fat bride into it!"

Buster's head smashed into the door and this time a chunk of fibre board flew off. He shoved his snout through the gap, gripping a piece of the splintering wood with his teeth.

"Then that ragamuffin urchin Clara phones me and asks for a job. She says she can produce any style of dress and then sends me a video. Do you know what she had been doing?"

Buster's head poked through a hole in the door. It wasn't big enough to get more than his nose and one eye through, but he was getting there.

Seeing me, he barked, *"Heeeere's Johnny!"*

Hopped up on adrenaline and terrified beyond belief, I shouted at him, "This is not time for Jack Nicholson quotes! Get in here and help me!"

My remark stalled Rudyard for a moment as he attempted to decipher what I was talking about. All he'd heard was my dog growling. He flicked his eyes across the room to check whether Buster was going to be a problem, decided he still had time to kill me and lunged.

I squealed and ran, ducking his swinging arm as I threw myself toward the front door.

I got within three feet, but no closer. Rudyard slammed into me, knocking me from my feet to sprawl on the carpet near Justin's desk. I got carpet burns on my hands from trying to stop myself, and hit my head on the desk as I scrambled to get away.

"*I suppose you would like some help*," remarked Amber.

I shot my head around to find her sitting halfway down the stairs. She was watching what was happening with the same level of interest she gives to all human interactions: almost none.

"Amber help me!"

Rudyard grabbed for my feet. I kicked and kicked, knocking his hands away and rolling to get behind the desk.

"Were you just asking your cat for help, Felicity?" he had an amused expression. "It's okay for a person to talk to their pets, but trying to have a conversation? That's borderline crazy right there."

Amber licked a paw. "*I believe we need to renegotiate my fish quota.*" she licked the paw again. "*Probably my chicken quota too. Also, I've never had lobster, but I hear it's very good.*"

"Amber!"

Rudyard grabbed Justin's desk, dispelling any hope I had of keeping it between us, by flipping it lengthways. It smashed into the staircase.

I had half a second to panic. After that, Rudyard had his hands on my throat and was squeezing.

"I asked if you knew what Clara had been doing? I can still scarcely believe it myself. That dressmaker's assistant had been making copies of my dress. Can you believe that?"

He was speaking calmly like we were having a chat at a garden party. Spots started to dance in my eyes as my brain was starved of oxygen. I clawed at his fingers, but I wasn't going to break his hold on me.

"Obviously, she had to die. Apart from anything else, she was too good. Far too good to be allowed to continue working. She never saw it coming. I waited outside her house thinking I could tail her wherever she was going and kill her then, but when she got on a bicycle ... well, that just made things easy."

I was struggling to hear what he was saying now; there was a clanging sound coming from inside my head. The pain from his hands on my throat was fading along with everything else and I felt a sort of peacefulness descend.

Then the back of my head hit something, the pain of it jolting me, and my senses returned. Rudyard was screaming and swearing, battling to get Amber off his face as she spat and clawed at him.

Gasping huge lungfuls of air, I wanted to get up. This was my chance, but my body didn't feel like obeying my commands right now. It thought having a rest or perhaps a little nap was in order.

I got an arm under my body and pushed myself upright.

Rudyard yelled in triumph, hauling Amber into the air with one hand gripping the scruff of her neck. She swore, making a terrible low sound in her throat.

Staggering, I got to my feet. I was going to fight, I just needed something to use as a weapon.

Buster's head smashed into the door again. The hole was now large enough for his whole head to fit through, but his shoulders needed a few more inches of space or they would jam.

Rudyard saw me get to my feet. His face was a mess, dozens of fine cuts where Amber's claws had raked his skin to cleave it open were running with bright red blood.

"I've changed my mind, Felicity," he sneered with heaving breaths. "I'm not sorry I have to kill you. I'm going to kill your cat first though."

From the wreckage of Justin's desk strewn across the floor, I selected a pair of scissors and brandished them with a lot more confidence than I felt.

"What are you going to do with those, Felicity?" Rudyard laughed at me. "Scissor me to death?"

He raised his arm as high as it would go, making me gasp in horror as I saw what he was going to do.

Out of options, probably about to die anyway, and overcome with a need to protect Amber, I screamed like a crazy woman and ran at him.

Buster chose that moment to smash through the door, one corner snapping off completely as he barrelled through it.

"No one kills that cat but me!"

Rudyard's arm had just started its descent. He was planning to smash Amber on the floor, a manoeuvre that would surely kill her instantly, but seeing my charge and hearing Buster's claws on the carpet again, he switched tactic.

He threw Amber at me. Terrified, the out-of-control Ragdoll tried to adjust her trajectory and body position so her paws were facing the right way.

On impulse, I threw the scissors. I didn't even look where they were going, I just knew I needed to have my hands free to catch Amber.

Buster yelled, *"Dun, dun, DAH!"* the furry tan and white blob whizzing across the edge of my vision as he rocketed toward Rudyard.

I caught Amber like a high rugby ball coming back to earth, folding my arms upward to clasp her to my chest. I then screamed in pain as all her claws went through my top and into my flesh – Amber was holding on for dear life.

Rudyard was screaming too, his left leg gripped tightly in Buster's mouth. My dog threw his weight to one side with a snarl, tearing flesh no doubt, but when Rudyard lost his footing and fell, his focus wasn't on the dog, but on the pair of scissors sticking out of his chest.

"Buster, enough." I made my tone as commanding as I could though my voice carried a tremble I felt right through my body.

Buster paused, twisting his head to one side enough that he could see where I was.

"Enough, now," I repeated my command.

He spat out Rudyard's leg, eliciting a whimper of pain from its owner, and sat back onto his haunches, panting.

"*That was fun,*" Buster managed between huffing breaths.

Rudyard had his hands around the scissors, his grip reversed so he could pull away from his body.

"I wouldn't do that if I were you," I warned. "There isn't much blood, but I think that's because they are acting as a plug. If you take them out …"

Rudyard lifted his head to look at me, and I got to watch his eyes roll back into his skull as he lost consciousness. I feared for a moment that he might be dead, but his chest continued to rise and fall steadily.

On unsteady legs, I walked around the office to get to my phone. I'd dropped it when he first lunged for me and had to search for it. Mercifully, it was in one piece and worked just fine when I dialled three nines and waited for it to connect.

Aftermath

The first squad car to arrive pulled up right outside the front door of my office, two familiar faces illuminated inside when the doors opened, and the interior light came on.

I waved to them through the glass, unable to work out what emotion my face ought to be displaying.

Constables Hardacre and Woods donned their hats and came inside, both looking around at the destruction that was my office and down at Rudyard who still occupied the same spot where he'd fallen.

He'd regained consciousness, but wasn't going to attempt to go anywhere, Buster saw to that, growling a warning every time Rudyard so much as twitched.

Plus, I think Rudyard was truly concerned about the scissors sticking out from between his ribs.

"Mrs, Philips, you sure do seem to get about," observed Constable Hardacre.

Patience saw Buster again and instantly fell into her routine of cooing and stroking him. There was blood in the fur around his ears where he cut himself trying to force his way through the door, but he wasn't hurt. If anything, he was happy to have picked up a few wounds to demonstrate how extreme the battle had been.

Just like yesterday, there were sirens wailing in the distance and coming closer. An ambulance arrived next.

Third on the scene was Mindy, arriving with my sister, Ginny, who couldn't believe her eyes. I'd called Mindy the moment I got off the line to the police. I wanted her to collect Amber and Buster. It was way past their dinner time, and it wasn't as though the police would want to take statements from them.

Mindy checked that I was okay, getting a weary smile in return. Truthfully, I was fine. I wanted that bath more than ever, and there wasn't a force on earth that was going to stop me having more wine than I ought to tonight. That was just personal stuff to ease my body though. The big stuff like me being alive and the people I cared about being alive, those boxes were ticked so how could I complain?

Vince appeared just as Mindy was getting ready to leave. She'd asked if she should stay with me and drive me home about a dozen times by then. Amber knew there was a piece of tuna waiting for her and was getting impatient.

I hadn't called Vince and still wasn't sure what to feel about him. He was a sort of loveable rogue, but how long would that last if I did start a relationship with him? Once we were something more than friends and a few weeks or months had passed, would he then be less romantically inclined and more of an annoyance?

I couldn't guess and it wasn't something I had the brain capacity to think about right now.

He was stopped outside by a cop positioned there to do specifically that, but I called out for him to be allowed through. His police scanner guy had heard dispatch sending officers to my building, he claimed. It was probably true, I decided. It was that or he was spying on me.

I was sitting in the comfy seat zone in the corner of my office, a blanket over my shoulders courtesy of the police and in deference to the door being open most of the time. I had a hot cup of tea in my belly, the empty cup now cooling on the coffee table.

Vince sat opposite me. "I wish I had been here to keep you safe."

I raised my hands to either side. "Not a scratch on me."

He cocked an eyebrow. "You have bruises on your neck."

Okay, he had me there.

"The paramedics said I would be fine." I was playing it down because my throat actually hurt. There was nothing anyone could do to fix it though. I had some paracetamol to take, and the bruising would fade in a few days.

Vince asked, "You want to tell me what happened?"

I'd already been through it with DS Wishaw and again with Mindy and my sister. I knew I would go through it again tomorrow when I visited the station to give a formal statement. I was still to provide one regarding Annabelle as I was the one who discovered her body.

I walked him through it though, explaining about the fake messages Rudyard sent to create his alibi. I told him about Gertrude and the code I'd been able to crack, about poor Clara and how talented she was. While the paramedics had been making Rudyard stable for transport – they said the scissors had punctured his lung – he admitted to killing Gertrude too.

When he knocked Clara off her bike and ran over her, he stopped and went back to make sure she was dead. Trying to cover his tracks, he picked up her phone, erasing the messages she had sent him and his replies. That was when he spotted the message to Gertrude Blithe-Leatham. She had the real dress and Rudyard wanted it back. Clara stole it from my office and flogged it to her.

I couldn't make sense of it because of all the brides, Gertrude was the one who hadn't even tried to slim down to fit in it. Of course, she was also having an affair with a pilot who she would meet for a cheeky shag while planning to marry someone else. She had been a complex woman.

Rudyard called Gertrude, told her he wanted to help her with the dress and killed her so he could get it back. Only once she was dead did he realise that taking it would look suspicious and potentially provide the evidence that would convict him if the police ever came snooping.

Three deaths all for the sake of a dress.

The police were not detaining me at the scene – they got what they wanted from me not long after they arrived, and I could have left as soon as the paramedics had checked me over. Why had I chosen to stay? I smiled to myself when I admitted the answer inside my own head.

I had wanted to see if Vince would show up.

The End

AUTHOR'S NOTE

Hello Dear Reader,

Thank you for reading this book. Is it the first of my books, or have you read dozens prior to this, I wonder? I figure there must be a blend of both, so just in case this is the first time you have ever read one of my cozy mystery adventures, I have big secret to reveal – I have lots more and they are all interlinked.

Felicity and her characters first appeared around a year ago when I introduced them in a series about a middle-aged sleuth called Patricia Fisher. Mrs Fisher is the woman who changed my life. I wasn't always a writer, you see. I was in the British Army for many years, and when I left that life, I moved into the corporate world.

When I published the first book in 2017, I had no idea it was going to go on to sell so many copies. That wasn't Patricia though, it was a story about an accidental paranormal detective. I was ten books into that series when I started writing Patricia and that was where things began to take off.

Patricia found herself working alongside the paranormal detective when she was handed a case that was a little too spooky for her, and then when she attended a wedding and met with a mystery to solve there, the wedding planner was Felicity. Another series – my fastest selling to date – stars a retired senior police detective and his former police dog. Albert and Rex also first appeared in a Patricia Fisher story and there are many other characters who flit between the different series, all crossing over and linking up to solve the various crimes I dream up.

So if you enjoyed this mystery tale and want more, you need to go all the way back to the start and pick a series to delve into. They were written, and still are, to be read simultaneously. I don't mean you need four or five books open at one time. No, what I mean is you can read Patricia and then Blue Moon (the paranormal detective series), then shift to Albert and Rex and then back to Felicity. That's how I wrote them.

There is a chronological order recorded on a few websites if that is something you need.

In this book I touch on the subject of sizeism and body shaming. It's not a topic I want to dive into or dwell on, but I do wish to state that I raise my children to be free of any prejudice. I hope there are more like me and that future generations allow the people around them to be who they are without offering opinion or comment.

Felicity speaks about the wedding industry in a negative manner with regards to sizeism, but I employed that opinion to fuel the story, not to attack the wedding industry, about which I know next to nothing. Upon researching wedding dresses, I found most websites catered for all shapes and sizes.

I make a joke out of in-car voice recognition systems because they are something that has plagued me. I was thoroughly impressed when I was appointed to the Board of Directors at a multi-million-dollar engineering firm and got a top end BMW to drive as my company car, but the clever stuff inside would dial anyone but the person I wanted. Whether this was me – when voice recognition software first started appearing for home use thirty years ago, I found my voice was simply too deep for it to pick up – or if everyone suffers equally, I cannot say.

I need to end this now as I can hear Albert and Rex calling. They have just arrived in my home county where they are on the trail of a hidden supervillain few even believe exists. I need to stop them getting into too much trouble.

Take care.

Steve Higgs

WHaT's neXT FoR FeLICITY

Wedding Ceremony Woes

It's the day of the wedding and the bride's little dog has gone missing. Champagne, her champion Pomeranian is to be the ring bearer and she will not get married without him.

Thus starts a day Felicity would sooner forget.

It's a mercy she has Amber and Buster with her. Sending them to scour the venue for the little dog, it's not long before the next problem arises.

Is the wedding just suffering a run of bad luck, or are there other forces in play?

Missing dogs and stressed-out brides are not the only thing on Felicity's mind – tonight is the deadline for the palace to announce who has been given the contract for the forthcoming royal wedding.

Felicity knows in her heart she is going to get it, but until she gets that phone call …

Get ready for high drama and high jinks – it's wedding time again!

WEDDING CEREMONY WOES

STEVE HIGGS

<h1 style="text-align:center"><u>More Books By Steve Higgs</u></h1>

Blue Moon Investigations
Paranormal Nonsense
The Phantom of Barker Mill
Amanda Harper Paranormal Detective
The Klowns of Kent
Dead Pirates of Cawsand
In the Doodoo With Voodoo
The Witches of East Malling
Crop Circles, Cows and Crazy Aliens
Whispers in the Rigging
Bloodlust Blonde – a short story
Paws of the Yeti
Under a Blue Moon – A Paranormal
Detective Origin Story
Night Work
Lord Hale's Monster
The Herne Bay Howlers
Undead Incorporated
The Ghoul of Christmas Past
The Sandman
Jailhouse Golem
Shadow in the Mine

Felicity Philips Investigates
To Love and to Perish
Tying the Noose
Aisle Kill Him
A Dress to Die For

Patricia Fisher Cruise Mysteries
The Missing Sapphire of Zangrabar
The Kidnapped Bride
The Director's Cut
The Couple in Cabin 2124
Doctor Death
Murder on the Dancefloor
Mission for the Maharaja
A Sleuth and her Dachshund in Athens
The Maltese Parrot
No Place Like Home

Patricia Fisher Mystery Adventures
What Sam Knew
Solstice Goat
Recipe for Murder
A Banshee and a Bookshop
Diamonds, Dinner Jackets, and Death
Frozen Vengeance
Mug Shot
The Godmother
Murder is an Artform
Wonderful Weddings and Deadly
Divorces
Dangerous Creatures

Patricia Fisher: Ship's Detective Series
The Ship's Detective
Fitness Can Kill
Death by Pirates

Albert Smith Culinary Capers
Pork Pie Pandemonium
Bakewell Tart Bludgeoning
Stilton Slaughter
Bedfordshire Clanger Calamity
Death of a Yorkshire Pudding
Cumberland Sausage Shocker
Arbroath Smokie Slaying
Dundee Cake Dispatch
Lancashire Hotpot Peril
Blackpool Rock Bloodshed
Kent Coast Oyster Obliteration

Realm of False Gods
Untethered magic
Unleashed Magic
Early Shift
Damaged but Powerful
Demon Bound
Familiar Territory
The Armour of God
Live and Die by Magic
Terrible Secrets

ABOUT THE AUTHOR

At school, the author was mostly disinterested in every subject except creative writing, for which, at age ten, he won his first award. However, calling it his first award suggests that there have been more, which there have not. Accolades may come but, in the meantime, he is having a ball writing mystery stories and crime thrillers and claims to have more than a hundred books forming an unruly queue in his head as they clamour to get out. He lives in the south-east corner of England with a duo of lazy sausage dogs. Surrounded by rolling hills, brooding castles, and vineyards, he doubts he will ever leave, the beer is just too good.

f facebook.com/stevehiggsauthor

g https://stevehiggsbooks.com/

www.ingramcontent.com/pod-product-compliance
Lightning Source LLC
Chambersburg PA
CBHW051008180726
48291CB00006B/2017